About the Author

David Almond's debut novel *Skellig* is one of the most remarkable children's novels published in recent years. It won the 1998 Whitbread Children's Book of the Year and the Carnegie Medal, and was shortlisted for the Guardian Children's Fiction Award. *Kit's Wilderness* is his second novel for children. His third, *Heaven Eyes*, is being published in early 2000.

'I grew up in a big family in a small steep town overlooking the River Tyne. It was a place of ancient coal mines, dark terraced streets, strange shops, new estates and wild heather hills. Our lives were filled with mysterious and unexpected events, and the place and its people have given me many of my stories. I always wanted to be a writer, though I told very few people until I was 'grown up'. I've been a postman, a brush salesman, an editor and a teacher. I've lived by the North Sea, in inner Manchester, in a Suffolk farmhouse, and I wrote my first stories in a remote and dilapidated Norfolk mansion.

Writing can be difficult, but sometimes it really does feel like a kind of magic. I think that stories are living things – among the most important things in the world.'

David Almond

Also published by Hodder Children's Books

The Fated Sky
Chance of Safety
Henrietta Branford

Hauntings
Nightcomers
Susan Price

Blackthorn, Whitethorn
Rachel Anderson

The Apostle Bird
Garry Disher

Waterbound
Secret Songs
Jane Stemp

Skellig

David Almond

Hodder
Children's
Books

a division of Hodder Headline plc

First published in Great Britain in 1998
by Hodder Children's Books

30 29 28 27 26 25 24 23 22 21

A Catalogue record for this book is available
from the British Library

ISBN 0 340 71600 2

Typeset by Avon Dataset Ltd, Bidford-on-Avon, Warks

Printed and bound in Great Britain by
Clays Ltd, St Ives plc

Hodder Children's Books
A Division of Hodder Headline plc
338 Euston Road
London NW1 3BH

For Freya Grace

One

I found him in the garage on a Sunday afternoon. It was the day after we moved into Falconer Road. The winter was ending. Mum had said we'd be moving just in time for the spring. Nobody else was there. Just me. The others were inside the house with Doctor Death, worrying about the baby.

He was lying there in the darkness behind the tea chests, in the dust and dirt. It was as if he'd been there forever. He was filthy and pale and dried out and I thought he was dead. I couldn't have been more wrong. I'd soon begin to see the truth about him, that there'd never been another creature like him in the world.

We called it the garage because that's what the estate agent, Mr Stone, called it. It was more like a demolition site or a rubbish dump or like one of those ancient warehouses they keep pulling down at the quay. Stone led us down the garden, tugged the door open and shone his little torch into the gloom. We shoved our heads in at the doorway with him.

'You have to see it with your mind's eye,' he said. 'See it cleaned, with new doors and the roof repaired. See it as a wonderful two-car garage.'

He looked at me with a stupid grin on his face.

'Or something for you, lad – a hideaway for you and your mates. What about that, eh?'

I looked away. I didn't want anything to do with him. All the way round the house it had been the same. Just see it in your mind's eye. Just imagine what could be done. All the way round I kept thinking of the old man, Ernie Myers, that had lived here on his own for years. He'd been dead nearly a week before they found him under the table in the kitchen. That's what I saw when Stone told us about seeing with the mind's eye. He even said it when we got to the dining room and there was an old cracked toilet sitting there in the corner behind a plywood screen. I just wanted him to shut up, but he whispered that towards the end Ernie couldn't manage the stairs. His bed was brought in here and a toilet was put in so everything was easy for him. Stone looked at me like he didn't think I should know about such things. I wanted to get out, to get back to our old house again, but Mum and Dad took it all in. They went on like it was going to be some big adventure. They bought the house. They started cleaning it and scrubbing it and painting it. Then the baby came too early. And here we were.

Two

I nearly got into the garage that Sunday morning. I took my own torch and shone it in. The outside doors to the back lane must have fallen off years ago and there were dozens of massive planks nailed across the entrance. The timbers holding the roof were rotten and the roof was sagging in. The bits of the floor you could see between the rubbish were full of cracks and holes. The people that took the rubbish out of the house were supposed to take it out of the garage as well, but they took one look at the place and said they wouldn't go in it even for danger money. There were old chests of drawers and broken wash-basins and bags of cement, ancient doors leaning against the walls, deck chairs with the cloth seats rotted away. Great rolls of rope and cable hung from nails. Heaps of water pipes and great boxes of rusty nails were scattered on the floor. Everything was covered in dust and spiders' webs. There was mortar that had fallen from the walls. There was a little window in one of the walls but it was filthy and there were rolls of cracked lino standing in front of it. The place stank of rot and dust. Even the bricks were crumbling like they couldn't bear the weight any more. It was like the whole thing was sick of itself and would collapse in a heap and have to get bulldozed away.

I heard something scratching in one of the corners, and something scuttling about, then it all stopped and it was just dead quiet in there.

I stood daring myself to go in.

I was just going to slip inside when I heard Mum shouting at me.

'Michael! What you doing?'

She was at the back door.

'Didn't we tell you to wait till we're sure it's safe?'

I stepped back and looked at her.

'Well, didn't we?' she shouted.

'Yes,' I said.

'So keep out! All right?'

I shoved the door and it lurched half-shut on its single hinge.

'All right?' she yelled.

'All right.' I said. 'Yes. All right. All right.'

'Do you not think we've got more to worry about than stupid you getting crushed in a stupid garage?'

'Yes.'

'You just keep out, then! Right?'

'Right. Right, right, right.'

Then I went back into the wilderness we called a garden and she went back to the flaming baby.

Three

The garden was another place that was supposed to be wonderful. There were going to be benches and a table and a swing. There were going to be goalposts painted on one of the walls by the house. There was going to be a pond with fish and frogs in it. But there was none of that. There were just nettles and thistles and weeds and half-bricks and lumps of stone. I stood there kicking the heads off a million dandelions.

After a while, Mum shouted was I coming in for lunch and I said no, I was staying out in the garden. She brought me a sandwich and a can of Coke.

'Sorry it's all so rotten and we're all in such rotten moods,' she said.

She touched my arm.

'You understand, though. Don't you, Michael? Don't you?'

I shrugged.

'Yes,' I said.

She touched me again and sighed.

'It'll be great again when everything's sorted out,' she said.

I sat on a pile of bricks against the house wall. I ate the sandwich and drank the Coke. I thought of Random Road where we'd come from, and all my old mates like Leakey and Coot. They'd be up on the top field now, playing a match that'd last all day.

Then I heard the doorbell ringing, and heard Doctor Death coming in. I called him Doctor Death because his face was grey and there were black spots on his hands and he didn't know how to smile. I'd seen him lighting up a fag in his car one day as he drove away from our door. They told me to call him Doctor Dan, and I did when I had to speak to him, but inside he was Doctor Death to me, and it fitted him much better.

I finished the Coke, waited a minute, then I went down to the garage again. I didn't have time to dare myself or to stand there listening to the scratching. I switched the torch on, took a deep breath, and tiptoed straight inside.

Something little and black scuttled across the floor. The door creaked and cracked for a moment before it was still. Dust poured through the torch beam. Something scratched and scratched in a corner. I tiptoed further in and felt spider webs breaking on my brow. Everything was packed in tight – ancient furniture, kitchen units, rolled-up carpets, pipes and crates and planks. I kept ducking down under the hose-pipes and ropes and kitbags that hung from the roof. More cobwebs snapped on my clothes and skin. The floor was broken and crumbly. I opened a cupboard an inch, shone the torch in and saw a million woodlice scattering away. I peered down into a great stone jar and saw the bones of some little animal that had died in there. Dead bluebottles were everywhere. There were ancient newspapers and magazines. I shone the torch on to one and saw that it came from nearly fifty years ago. I moved so carefully. I was scared every moment that the whole thing was going to collapse. There was dust clogging my throat and nose. I knew they'd be yelling for me soon and I knew I'd better get out. I leaned across a heap of tea chests and shone the torch into the space behind and that's when I saw him.

I thought he was dead. He was sitting with his legs stretched out, and his head tipped back against the wall. He was covered in dust and webs like everything else and his face was thin and pale. Dead bluebottles were scattered on his hair and shoulders. I shone the torch on his white face and his black suit.

'What do you want?' he said.

He opened his eyes and looked up at me.

His voice squeaked like he hadn't used it in years.

'What do you want?'

My heart thudded and thundered.

'I said, what do you want?'

Then I heard them yelling for me from the house.

'Michael! Michael! Michael!'

I shuffled out again. I backed out through the door.

It was Dad. He came down the path to me.

'Didn't we tell you—' he started.

'Yes,' I said. 'Yes. Yes.'

I started to brush the dust off myself. A spider dropped away from my chin on a long string.

He put his arm around me.

'It's for your own good,' he said.

He picked a dead bluebottle out of my hair.

He thumped the side of the garage and the whole thing shuddered.

'See?' he said. 'Imagine what might happen.'

I grabbed his arm to stop him thumping it again.

'Don't,' I said. 'It's all right. I understand.'

He squeezed my shoulder and said everything would be better soon.

He laughed.

'Get all that dust off before your mother sees, eh?'

Four

I hardly slept that night. Every time I did drop off I saw him coming out of the garage door and coming through the wilderness to the house. I saw him in my bedroom. I saw him come right to the bed. He stood there all dusty and white with the dead bluebottles all over him.

'What do you want?' he whispered. 'I said, what do you want?'

I told myself I was stupid. I'd never seen him at all. That had all been part of a dream as well. I lay there in the dark. I heard Dad snoring and when I listened hard I could hear the baby breathing. Her breathing was cracked and hissy. In the middle of the night when it was pitch black I dropped off again but she started bawling. I heard Mum getting up to feed her. I heard Mum's voice cooing and comforting. Then there was just silence again, and Dad snoring again. I listened hard for the baby again and I couldn't hear her.

It was already getting light when I got up and tiptoed into their room. Her cot was beside their bed. They were lying fast asleep with their arms around each other. I looked down at the baby. I slipped my hand under the covers and touched her. I could feel her heart beating fast. I could feel the thin rattle of her breath, and her chest rising and falling. I felt how hot it was in there, how soft her bones were, how tiny she was. There was a dribble of spit and milk on her neck. I wondered if she was going to die. They'd been scared about that in the hospital. Before they let her come home she'd been in a glass case with tubes and wires sticking in her and we'd stood around staring in like she was in a fish tank.

I took my hand away and tucked the covers around her again. Her face was dead white and her hair was dead black. They'd told me I had to keep praying for her but I didn't know what to pray.

'Hurry up and get strong if you're going to,' I whispered.

Mum half woke up and saw me there.

'What d'you want, love?' she whispered.

She stretched her hand out of the bed towards me.

'Nothing,' I whispered, and tiptoed back to my room.

I looked down into the wilderness. There was a blackbird singing away on the garage roof. I thought of him lying behind the tea chests with the cobwebs in his hair. What was he doing there?

Five

I asked them at breakfast what was going to happen to the garage now.

'When they coming to clear it out?' I said.

Mum clicked her tongue and sighed and looked up at the ceiling.

'When we can get somebody to come,' said Dad. 'It's not important, son. Not now.'

'OK,' I said.

He was going to be off work today so he could get on with the house. Mum was taking the baby for more check-ups at the hospital.

'Should I stay off so I can help?' I said.

'Yes,' he said. 'You can take Ernie's toilet out and scrub the floorboards round it.'

'I'll go to school,' I said.

And I shoved my packed lunch into my sack and headed out.

Before we moved, they asked me if I wanted to move school

as well, but I didn't. I wanted to stay at Kenny Street High with Leakey and Coot. I didn't mind that I'd have to get the bus through town. That morning I told myself that it gave me time to think about what was going on. I tried to think about it but I couldn't think. I watched the people getting on and off. I looked at them reading their papers or picking their nails or looking dreamily out of the windows. I thought how you could never tell just by looking at them what they were thinking or what was happening in their lives. Even when you got daft people or drunk people on buses, people that went on stupid and shouted rubbish or tried to tell you all about themselves, you could never really tell about them either.

I wanted to stand up and say, 'There's a man in our garage and my sister is ill and it's the first day I've travelled from the new house to the old school.'

But I didn't. I just went on looking at all the faces and swinging back and forward when the bus swung round corners. I knew if somebody looked at me, they'd know nothing about me, either.

It was strange being at school again. Loads had happened to me, but school stayed just the same. Rasputin still asked us to lift up our hearts and voices and sing out loud in assembly. The Yeti yelled at us to keep to the left in the corridors. Monkey Mitford went red in the face and stamped his feet when we didn't know our fractions. Miss Clarts got tears in her eyes when she told us the story of Icarus, how his wings had melted when he flew too close to the sun, and how he had dropped like a stone past his father Daedelus into the sea. At lunchtime, Leakey and Coot argued for ages about whether a shot had gone over the line.

I couldn't be bothered with it all.

I went to the fence at the edge of the field and stared over the town towards where I lived now.

While I was standing there, Mrs Dando, one of the auxiliaries, came over to me. She'd known my parents for years.

'You OK, Michael?' she said.

'Fine.'

'And the baby?'

'Fine, too.'

'Not footballing today?'

I shook my head.

'Tell your parents I was asking,' she said.

She took a fruit gum out of her pocket and held it out to me. A fruit gum. It was what she gave the new kids when they were sad or something.

'Just for you,' she whispered, and she winked.

'No,' I said. 'No, thanks.'

And I ran back and did a brilliant sliding tackle on Coot.

All day I wondered about telling somebody what I'd seen, but I told nobody. I said to myself it had just been a dream. It must have been.

Six

At home, there was a hole in the floor where Ernie's toilet had been. It was filled with new cement. The plywood screen had gone. Ernie's old gas fire had been taken away and there was just a square black gap behind the hearth. The floor was soaking wet and it stank of disinfectant. Dad was filthy and wet and grinning. He took me into the wilderness. The toilet was standing there in the middle of the thistles and weeds.

'Thought it'd make a nice garden seat for us,' he said.

The gas fire and the plywood were down by the garage door, but they hadn't been taken inside.

He looked at me and winked. 'Come and see what I found.'

He led me down to the garage door.

'Hold your nose,' he said. He bent down and started to open a newspaper parcel. 'Ready?'

It was a parcel of birds. Four of them.

'Found them behind the fire,' he said. 'Must have got stuck in the chimney and couldn't get out again.'

You could make out that three of them were pigeons because of their grey and white feathers. The last one was pigeon-shaped, but it was all black.

'This was the last one I found,' he said. 'It was under a heap of soot and dust that had fallen down the chimney.'

'Is it a pigeon as well?'

'Yes. Been there a long, long time, that's all.'

He took my hand.

'Touch it,' he said. 'Feel it. Go on, it's OK.'

I let him hold my fingers against the bird. It was hard as stone. Even the feathers were hard as stone.

'Been there so long it's nearly a fossil,' he said.

'It's hard as stone,' I said.

'That's right. Hard as stone.'

I went and washed my hands in the kitchen.

'Today was OK?' he said.

'Yes. Leakey and Coot said they might come over on Sunday.'

'That's good. You managed the buses OK, then?'

I nodded.

'Might be able to drive you there next week,' he said. 'Once we're sorted out a bit.'

'It's OK,' I said. 'Mrs Dando asked about the baby.'

'You told her she was fine?'

'Yes,' I said.

'Good. Get some Coke and a sandwich or something. I'll make tea when the others come home.'

Then he went upstairs to have a bath.

I looked down through the wilderness. I waited for ages, listening to Dad's bathwater banging its way through the pipes. I got my torch off the kitchen shelf. My hands were trembling. I went out, past Ernie's toilet, the fire, and the dead pigeons. I stood at the garage door and switched the torch on. I took a deep breath and tiptoed inside. I felt the cobwebs and the dust and I imagined that the whole thing would collapse. I heard things scuttling and scratching. I edged past the rubbish and the ancient furniture and my heart was thudding and thundering. I told myself I was stupid. I told myself I'd been dreaming. I told myself I wouldn't see him again.

But I did.

Seven

I leaned over the tea chests and shone the torch and there he was. He hadn't moved. He opened his eyes and closed them again.

'You again,' he said, in his cracked, squeaky voice.

'What you doing there?' I whispered.

He sighed, like he was sick to death of everything.

'Nothing,' he squeaked. 'Nothing, nothing, and nothing.'

I watched a spider scrambling across his face. He caught it in his fingers and popped it in his mouth.

'They're coming to clear the rubbish out,' I said. 'And the whole place could collapse.'

He sighed again.

'Got an aspirin?'

'An aspirin?'

'Never mind.'

His face was pale as dry plaster. His black suit hung like a sack on his thin bones.

My heart pounded. The dust was clogging my nostrils and throat. I chewed my lips and watched him.

'You're not Ernie Myers, are you?' I said.

'That old git? Coughing his guts and spewing everywhere?'

'Sorry,' I whispered.

'What do you want?' he said.

'Nothing.'

'You got an aspirin?'

'No.'

'Thanks very much.'

'What will you do?' I said. 'They'll clear the place out. It'll all collapse. What'll . . .'

'Nothing. Go away.'

I listened for noises from outside, for them calling me.

'You could come inside,' I said.

He laughed, but he didn't smile.

'Go away,' he whispered.

He picked a bluebottle from the front of his suit and popped it in his mouth.

'Is there something I could bring you?' I said.

'An aspirin,' he squeaked.

'Something you'd like to eat?' I said.

'27 and 53.'

'What?'

'Nothing. Go away. Go away.'

I backed away, out into the light. I brushed the dust and bluebottles and cobwebs off. I looked up and saw Dad through the frosted glass of the bathroom window. I could just hear him singing 'The Black Hills of Dakota'.

'Are you the new boy here?' said somebody.

I turned round. There was a girl's head sticking up over the top of the wall into the back lane.

'Are you the new boy?' she repeated.

'Yes.'

'I'm Mina.'

I stared at her.

'Well?' she said.

'What?'

She clicked her tongue and shook her head and said in a bored-sounding singsong voice, 'I'm Mina. You're . . .'

'Michael,' I said.

'Good.'

Then she jumped back and I heard her land in the lane.

'Nice to meet you, Michael,' she said through the wall, then she ran away.

Eight

When he came down from his bath, Dad started moaning that there was no bread and there were no eggs, and in the end he said,

'I know. Let's have a takeaway, eh?'

It was like a light went on in my head.

He had the menu from the Chinese round the corner in his hand.

'We'll get it in for when your mum gets back,' he said. 'What d'you fancy?'

'27 and 53,' I said.

'That's clever,' he said. 'You did that without looking. What's your next trick?'

He wrote it all down.

'Special chow mein for Mum, spring rolls and pork char sui for you, beef and mushroom for me, crispy seaweed and prawn crackers for the baby. And if she won't eat them, we will and serve her right, eh? She'll be back on boring mother's milk again.'

He phoned the Chinese, gave me the cash, and I ran round

to collect it all. By the time I got back again, Mum and the baby were there. She tried to make a fuss of me and kept asking me about the journey and about school. Then the baby puked over her shoulder and she had to get cleaned up.

Dad belted through his beef and mushroom and the sea-weed and prawn crackers. He said he was all clogged up with Ernie's dust and he swigged off a bottle of beer. When he saw I was leaving half of mine, he reached over with his fork.

I covered it with my arm.

'You'll get fat,' I said.

Mum laughed.

'Fatt*er*!' she said.

'I'm famished,' he said. 'Worked like a bloomin' slave for you lot today.'

He reached out and tickled the baby's chin and kissed her.

'Specially for you, little chick.'

I kept my arm in front of the food.

'Fatso,' I said.

He lifted his shirt and grabbed his belly with his fingers.

'See?' said Mum.

He looked at us.

He dipped his finger into the sauce at the edge of my plate.

'Delicious,' he said. 'But enough's enough. I've had an ample sufficiency, thank you.'

Then he went to the fridge and got another beer and a great big lump of cheese.

I tipped what was left of 27 and 53 into the takeaway tin and put it in the outside bin.

Nine

I saw Mina again later that evening. I was in the little front garden with Dad. We stood there in the thistles and dandelions. He was telling me as usual how wonderful it would be – flowers here and a tree there and a bench under the front window. I saw her further along the street. She was in a tree in another front garden on the same side of the street as us. She was sitting on a fat branch. She had a book and a pencil in her hand. She kept sticking the pencil in her mouth and staring up into the tree.

'Wonder who that is.'

'She's called Mina.'

'Ah.'

She must have seen us looking at her but she didn't move.

Dad went in to check the cement in the dining room.

I went out the gate and along the street and looked up at Mina in the tree.

'What you doing up there?' I said.

She clicked her tongue.

'Silly you,' she said. 'You've scared it away. Typical.'

'Scared what away?'

'The blackbird.'

She put the book and the pencil in her mouth. She swung over the branch and dropped into the garden. She stood looking at me. She was little and she had hair as black as coal and the kind of eyes you think can see right through you.

'Never mind,' she said. 'It'll come again.'

She pointed up to the rooftop. The blackbird was up there, tipping its tail back and forward, and squawking.

'That's its warning call,' she said. 'It's telling its family there's danger near. Danger. That's you.'

She pointed up into the tree.

'If you climb up where I was and look along that branch there you'll see its nest. There's three tiny ones. But don't you dare go any nearer.'

She sat on the garden wall and faced me.

'This is where I live,' she said. 'Number Seven. You've got a baby sister.'

'Yes.'

'What's her name?'

'We haven't decided yet.'

She clicked her tongue and rolled her eyes towards the sky.

She opened her book.

'Look at this,' she said.

It was full of birds. Pencil drawings, lots of them coloured in blues and greens and reds.

'This is the blackbird,' she said. 'They're common, but nevertheless very beautiful. A sparrow. These are tits. And lovely chaffinches. And look, this is the goldfinch that visited last Thursday.'

She showed me the goldfinch, the greens and reds and bright yellows in it.

'My favourite,' she said.

She slapped the book shut.

'Do you like birds?' she said, and she looked at me as if something I'd done had made her cross.

'I don't know,' I said.

'Typical. Do you like drawing?'

'Sometimes.'

'Drawing makes you look at the world more closely. It helps you to see what you're looking at more clearly. Did you know that?'

I said nothing.

'What colour's a blackbird?' she said.

'Black.'

'Typical!'

She swung round into the garden.

'I'm going in,' she said. 'I look forward to seeing you again. I'd also like to see your baby sister if that can be arranged.'

Ten

I tried to stay awake that night, but it was hopeless. I was dreaming straight away. I dreamed that the baby was in the blackbird's nest in Mina's garden. The blackbird fed her on flies and spiders and she got stronger and stronger until she flew out of the tree and over the rooftops and on to the garage roof. Mina sat on the back wall drawing her. When I went closer, Mina whispered, 'Stay away. You're danger!'

Then the baby was bawling in the room next door and I woke up.

I lay listening to Mum cooing and comforting and the baby squeaking and hissing. The birds were singing outside. When the feed was over and I was sure everyone was asleep, I crept out of bed, got my torch, pulled some clothes on and tiptoed past their room. I took a jar of aspirin from the bathroom. I went downstairs, opened the back door and tiptoed into the wilderness.

The takeaway trays were down under newspapers and a heap of weeds. They'd tilted over and lots of the sauce had run out. When I looked inside the char sui was all gluey and red and cold. I dropped the soggy spring rolls into the same tray and went down towards the garage.

'You must be stupid,' I told myself. 'You must be going round the stupid bend.'

I looked up at the blackbird on the garage roof and saw how it opened its yellow beak so wide as it sang. I saw the sheens of gold and blue where the early light shone on its black.

I switched on the torch, took a deep breath, and stepped inside.

The scuttling and scratching started. Something skittered across my foot and I nearly dropped the food. I came to the tea chests and shone the torch behind.

'You again?' he squeaked. 'Thought you'd gone away.'

'I've brought something,' I said.

He opened his eyes and looked at me.

'Aspirin,' I said. 'And number 27 and 53. Spring rolls and pork char sui.'

He laughed but he didn't smile.

'Not as stupid as you look,' he squeaked.

I held the takeaway tray across the tea chests towards him. He took it in his hand but he started to wobble and I had to take it back again.

'No strength,' he squeaked.

I squeezed between the tea chests. I squatted down beside him. I held the tray up and shone the torch on to the food. He dipped his finger in. He licked his finger and groaned. He stuck his finger in again and hooked a long slimy string of beansprouts and sauce. He stuck his tongue out and licked. He slurped out pieces of pork and mushrooms. He shoved the spring rolls into his mouth. The red sauce trickled down from his lips, down over his chin on to his black jacket.

'Aaaah,' he said. 'Ooooooh.'

He sounded like he was loving it, or he was in pain, or both those things together. I held the tray closer to his chin. He dipped and licked and groaned.

His fingers were twisted and stunted. His knuckles were swollen.

'Put the aspirin in,' he said.

I put two aspirin in the sauce and he picked them out and swallowed them.

He belched and belched. His hand slipped to his side again. His head slumped back against the wall.

'Food of the gods,' he whispered. '27 and 53.'

I put the tray down on the floor beside him and shone the torch on him. There were hundreds of tiny creases and cracks all over his pale face. A few fine colourless hairs grew on his chin. The red sauce below his lips was like congealed blood. When he opened his eyes again, I saw the tiny red veins like a dark net across the whites of his eyes. There was a smell of dust, old clothes, dry sweat.

'Had a good look?' he whispered.

'Where you from?'

'Nowhere.'

'They'll clear all this out. What will you do?'

'Nothing.'

'What will you—'

'Nothing, nothing and nothing.'

He closed his eyes again.

'Leave the aspirin,' he said.

I took the top off, and put the jar on the floor. I had to push aside a little heap of hard furry balls. I held one up to the torchlight, and saw it was made of tiny bones glued together with fur and skin.

'What you looking at, eh?' he said.

I put it on the floor again.

'Nothing.'

The blackbird on the roof sang louder and louder.

'There's a doctor comes to see my sister,' I said. 'I could bring him here to see you.'

'No doctors. Nobody.'

'Who are you?'

'Nobody.'

'What can I do?'

'Nothing.'

'My baby sister's very ill.'

'Babies!'

'Is there anything you can do for her?'

'Babies! Spittle, muck, spew and tears.'

I sighed. It was hopeless.

'My name's Michael. I'm going now. Is there anything else I can bring you?'

'Nothing. 27 and 53.'

He belched again. His breath stank. Not just the Chinese

food, but the stench of the other dead things he ate: the bluebottles, the spiders. He made a gag noise in his throat and he leaned away from the wall like he was going to be sick. I put my hand beneath his shoulder to steady him. I felt something there, something held in by his jacket. He retched. I tried not to breathe, not to smell him. I reached across his back and felt something beneath his other shoulder as well. Like thin arms, folded up. Springy and flexible.

He retched, but he wasn't sick. He leaned back against the wall and I took my hand away.

'Who are you?' I said.

The blackbird sang and sang.

'I wouldn't tell anybody,' I said.

He lifted his hand and looked at it in the torchlight.

'I'm nearly nobody,' he said. 'Most of me is Arthur.'

He laughed but he didn't smile.

'Arthur Itis,' he squeaked. 'He's the one that's ruining me bones. Turns you to stone then crumbles you away.'

I touched his swollen knuckles.

'What's on your back?' I said.

'A jacket, then a bit of me, then lots and lots of Arthur.'

I tried to slip my hand beneath his shoulder again.

'No good,' he squeaked. 'Nothing there's no good no more.'

'I'm going,' I said. 'I'll keep them from clearing the place out. I'll bring you more. I won't bring Doctor Death.'

He licked the dry sauce from below his lips.

'27 and 53,' he said. '27 and 53.'

I left him, backed away towards the door, went out into the light. The blackbird flew away over the gardens, squawking. I tiptoed into the house. I stood for a minute at the baby's cot. I put my hand beneath the blankets and felt the rattling of her breath and how soft and warm she was. I felt how tender her bones were.

Mum looked up at me and I could tell she was still asleep.

'Hello,' she whispered.

I tiptoed back to bed.

When I slept, I dreamed that my bed was all twigs and leaves and feathers, just like a nest.

Eleven

Next morning, Dad said he could hardly move. He was all bent over. He said his back was killing him. He was stiff as a blinking board.

'Where's those aspirin?' he yelled down the stairs.

Mum laughed.

'All this exercise'll do him good,' she said. 'It'll get that fat off him.'

He yelled again:

'I said, where's those blooming aspirin?'

I kissed the baby and ran to catch the bus to school.

That morning, we had science with Rasputin. He showed us a poster of our ancestors, of the endless shape-changing that had led to us. There were monkeys and apes, the long line of ape-like creatures in between, then us. It showed how we began to stand straighter, how we lost most of our hair, how we began to use tools, how our heads changed shape to hold our big brains. Coot whispered it was all a load of rubbish. His Dad had told him there was no way that monkeys could turn into men. Just had to look at them. Stands to reason.

I asked Rasputin if we'd keep on changing shape and he said, 'Who knows, Michael? Maybe evolution will go on for ever. Maybe we'll go on changing for ever.'

'Bollocks,' whispered Coot.

We drew the skeleton of an ape and the skeleton of a man. I remembered what Mina had said and I looked really closely at the poster. I put my hand up and said, 'What are shoulder blades for, sir?'

Rasputin crinkled his face up. He reached behind his back and felt his shoulder blades and smiled.

'I know what my mother used to tell me,' he said. 'But to be honest, I really haven't got a clue.'

Afterwards, Coot hunched his shoulders up and lowered his head and stuck his chin out. He lurched through the corridor, grunting and running at the girls.

Lucy Carr started screaming.

'Stop it, you pig!' she said.

Coot just laughed.

'Pig?' said Coot. 'I'm not a pig. I'm a gorilla.'

And he ran at her again.

In the yard when I played football, I realised how tired I was with being awake so much during the night. Leakey kept asking what was the matter with me. I was playing crap. Mrs Dando came again when I was standing by myself at the side of the field.

'What's up?' she said.

'Nothing.'

'And how's the little one.'

'Fine.'

I looked at the ground.

'Sometimes I think she stops breathing,' I said. 'Then I look at her and she's fine.'

'She will be fine,' she said. 'You'll see. Babies so often bring worry with them into the world, but you'll be wrestling with her before you know where you are.'

She touched me on the shoulder. For a moment. I wondered about telling her about the man in the garage. Then I saw Leakey looking so I shrugged her off and I ran back, yelling,

'On me head! On me head!'

It was a dozy afternoon. Some easy Maths, then Miss Clarts reading us another story, this time about Ulysses and his men trapped in the cave with the one-eyed monster Polyphemus. I was nearly asleep as she told us how they had escaped by pretending to be sheep.

I took my skeleton picture home. I kept looking at it on the bus. There was an old bloke sitting beside me with a Jack Russell on his knee. He smelt of pee and pipesmoke.

'What's that?' he said.

'Picture of what we used to be like long ago,' I said.

'Can't say I remember that,' he said. 'And I'm pretty ancient.'

He started going on about how he'd seen a monkey in a circus in his young days. They'd trained it to make tea but it was nothing like a person, really. But maybe it had just been practising. There was spit dribbling at the side of his mouth. I could see he wasn't all there.

'There's a man in our garage,' I said when he'd shut up.

'Aye?' he said.

The Jack Russell yapped. He put his hand around its mouth. He seemed to be thinking hard.

'Aye,' he said again. 'And there was the loveliest lass on the trapeze. You could swear she could nearly fly.'

Twelve

Doctor Death was there when I got home. He was in the kitchen with Mum and Dad. He had the baby on his knee and he was fastening her vest up. He winked at me when I came in. Dad poked me in the ribs. I saw how flat Mum's face was.

'It's this damn place!' she said when Doctor Death had gone. 'How can she thrive when it's all so dirty and all in such a mess?'

She pointed out of the window.

'See what I mean?' she said. 'Bloody stupid toilet. Bloody ruins. A bloody stupid wilderness.'

She started crying. She said we should never have left Random Road. We should never have come to this stinking derelict place. She walked back and forward in the kitchen with the baby in her arms.

'My little girl,' she murmured. 'My poor little girl.'

'The baby has to go back to hospital,' Dad whispered. 'Just for a while. So the doctors can keep an eye on her. That's all. She'll be fine.'

He stared out of the window into the wilderness.

'I'll work harder,' he said. 'I'll get it all ready for when she comes back again.'

'I'll help,' I said, but he didn't seem to hear.

We had bread and cheese and tea. The baby lay there in a little carry cot beside us. Mum went upstairs to put together the things the baby would need in hospital. I put the skeleton picture on the table and looked at it but couldn't concentrate on it.

'That's good,' Dad said, but he wasn't looking at it properly, either.

I went up and sat on the landing. I watched Mum throwing vests and nappies and cardigans into a little case. She kept clicking her tongue, and going, 'Agh! Agh!' like she was mad at everything. She saw me there and tried to smile but started to click her tongue again.

When she was finished, she said, 'Don't worry. It won't be for long.'

She leaned down and put her hand on my head.

'What are shoulder blades for?' I said.

'Oh, Michael!' she said.

She shoved past me like I was really getting on her nerves. But when she was halfway down the stairs she stopped and came back to me. She slipped her fingers under my shoulder blades.

'They say that shoulder blades are where your wings were, when you were an angel,' she said. 'They say they're where your wings will grow again one day.'

'It's just a story, though,' I said. 'A fairy tale for little kids. Isn't it?'

'Who knows? But maybe one day we all had wings and one day we'll all have wings again.'

'D'you think the baby had wings?'

'Oh, I'm sure that one had wings. Just got to take one look at her. Sometimes I think she's never quite left Heaven and never quite made it all the way here to Earth.'

She smiled, but there were tears in her eyes.

'Maybe that's why she has such trouble staying here,' she said.

I watched her, wondered what she'd say if I told her now about the man in the garage. I didn't tell her.

Before she went away, I held the baby for a while. I touched her skin and her tiny soft bones. I felt the place where her wings had been. Then we went in the car to the hospital. We went to the baby's ward and left Mum and the baby there. Dad and I drove back to Falconer Road. We sat in the big empty house and looked at each other. Then he went back to painting the dining-room walls.

I drew a skeleton with wings rising from the shoulder blades.

I looked out of the window and saw Mina sitting high up, on top of the back wall.

Thirteen

'You're unhappy,' she said.

I stood there looking up at her.

'The baby's back in hospital,' I said.

She sighed. She gazed at a bird that was wheeling high above.

'It looks like she's going to bloody die,' I said.

She sighed again.

'Would you like me to take you somewhere?' she said.

'Somewhere?'

'Somewhere secret. Somewhere nobody knows about.'

I looked back at the house and saw Dad through the dining-room window. I looked at Mina and her eyes went right through me.

'Five minutes,' she said. 'He won't even know you're gone.'

I crossed my fingers.

'Come on,' she whispered, and I opened the gate and slipped out into the lane.

'Quickly,' she whispered, and she bent low and started to run.

At the end of the street she turned into another back lane. The houses behind the walls here were bigger and higher and older. The back gardens were longer and had tall trees in them. It was Crow Road.

She stopped outside a dark-green gate. She took a key from somewhere, unlocked it, slipped inside. I followed her in. Something brushed against my leg. I looked down and saw a cat that had come in through the gate with us.

'Whisper!' said Mina, and she grinned.

'What?'

'The cat's called Whisper. You'll see him everywhere.'

The house was blackened stone. The windows were boarded up. Mina ran to the door and opened it. There was a painted red sign over the door: DANGER.

'Take no notice,' she said. 'It's just to keep the vandals out.'

She stepped inside.

'Come on,' she whispered. 'Quickly!'

I went in, and Whisper entered at my side.

It was pitch black in there. I could see nothing. Mina took my hand.

'Don't stop,' she said, and she led me forward.

She led me up some wide stairs. As my eyes got used to the gloom I made out the shapes of the boarded windows, of dark doorways and broad landings. We ascended three stairways, passed three landings. Then the stairs narrowed and we came to a final narrow doorway.

'The attic,' she whispered. 'Stay very still in there. They

might not want you to be there. They might attack you!'

'What might?'

'How brave are you? They know me and they know Whisper but they don't know you. How brave are you? As brave as me?'

I stared at her. How could I know?

'You are,' she said. 'You have to be.'

She turned the handle. She held her breath. She took my hand again, led me inside, closed the door behind us. She hunched down on the floor. She pulled me down as well. The cat lay quietly at our side.

'Stay very still,' she whispered. 'Stay very quiet. Just watch.'

We were right inside the roof. It was a wide room with a sloping ceiling. The floorboards were split and uneven. Plaster had fallen from the walls. Light came in through an arched window that jutted out through the roof. Glass was scattered on the floor below the window. You could see the rooftops and steeples of the town through it, and the clouds, turning red as the day began to close.

I held my breath.

The room darkened and reddened as the sun went down.

'What will happen?' I whispered.

'Shh. Just watch. Wait and watch.'

Then she trembled.

'Look! Look!'

A pale bird rose from some corner of the room and flew silently to the window. It stood there, looking out. Then another came, wheeling once around the room, its wings beating within inches of our faces before it, too, settled before the window.

I didn't breathe. Mina gripped my hand. I watched the birds, the way their broad round faces turned to each other, the way their claws gripped the window frame. Then they went, flying silently out into the red dusk.

'Owls,' whispered Mina. 'Tawny owls!'

And she looked right into me again and laughed.

'Sometimes they'll attack intruders. But they saw you were with me. They knew you were OK.'

She pointed to the back wall, a gaping hole where some plaster and bricks had fallen in.

'That's the nest,' she said. 'There's chicks in there. Don't go near. They'll defend them to the death.'

She laughed at my stunned silence.

'Come on,' she whispered. 'Be quick!'

And we left the attic and ran down the broad stairs and out of the house and into the garden. She locked the door and the garden gate and we ran through the lanes to our wilderness.

'Tell nobody,' she whispered.

'No,' I said.

'Hope to die,' she said.

'What?'

'Cross your heart and hope to die.'

'Cross my heart and hope to die.'

'Good,' she said, and she ran away with Whisper at her heels.

I stepped back through our gate and there was Dad, beyond the dining-room window, stretching up to paint the walls.

Fourteen

I didn't go to school next day.

I was having breakfast with Dad when I started trembling for no reason. He put his arm around me.

'What about working with me today?' he asked.

I nodded.

'We'll get it all done for them, eh?' he said. 'You and me together.'

I heard him on the phone in the hall, talking to school.

'His sister . . .' I heard him say. 'Yes, so much all at once . . . State of distress . . . Yes, yes.'

I put some old jeans on. I stirred the green paint he was going to use on the dining-room walls. I laid old sheets on the floor.

'What should I do?' I asked, as he stepped up on to the stepladders.

He shrugged. He looked out through the window.

'How about getting some of that jungle cleared,' he said. He laughed. 'Get covered up first, though. And watch out for the tigers.'

I wore a pair of old gloves. I used an old pair of scissors to cut the stems that wouldn't snap. I dug down with a trowel to get at the roots. Thistle thorns stuck in my skin. There was green sap all over me. I made a big pile of weeds and a heap of stones against the house wall. I found spiders dangling from my hair and clothes. Shiny black beetles scurried away from me. Centipedes squirmed down into the loosened soil. As the morning went on I cleared a wider and wider space. Dad came out and we drank some juice together. We sat against the house wall, and watched blackbirds come to where I'd been working. They dug into the soil, collected worms and insects for their young, flew over the gardens and rooftops to their nests.

We talked about what we wanted to have out here: a pond, a fountain, a place Mum could sunbathe, somewhere to put the baby's playpen.

'We'll have to cover the pond once she's crawling,' he said. 'Don't want any dangers in her way.'

We went back to work again.

My arms were aching and my skin was stinging. Dust and pollen clogged my nose and throat. I crawled through the weeds, dug down into the earth, slashed and pulled at the stems. I dreamed of the baby crawling out here. She was strong and she kept on giggling and pointing at the birds. Then I saw how close to the garage I had crawled and I thought of the man in there, how he just sat there, how he seemed to be just waiting to die.

I stood up and went to the garage door. I stood listening.

There was nothing but the usual scuttling and scratching.

'You can't just sit there!' I called. 'You can't just sit like you're waiting to die!'

There was no answer. I stood listening.

'You can't!' I said.

No answer.

That afternoon, we went to the hospital. As we drove out of the street in the car, I saw Mina, sitting in the tree in her garden. She had a notebook in her lap and she was writing or drawing. She looked at us, and she waved, but she didn't smile.

'Strange one, that,' said Dad.

'Yes,' I murmured.

In the hospital, the baby was in a glass case again. There were wires and tubes going into her. She was fast asleep. Mum said everything was fine. The doctors had told her the baby could go home again in a day or two. We looked down through the glass and Mum put her arm around me. She saw the blotches on my skin. She asked the nurses for some cream and rubbed it gently into me.

The baby woke up and looked straight into my eyes and screwed up her face like she was smiling.

'See?' said Mum. 'She's going to get better for us. Aren't you, my little chick?'

She closed her eyes again. Mum said she would stay at the hospital tonight as well. Dad and I headed home.

'27 and 53 again?' he said as we drove through the traffic.

'Yes,' I said.

‘Right,’ he said. ‘A bit more work, then you can go round to the Chinese later.’

We drove into the street. Mina was sitting on the low wall to her front garden, reading a book. She watched us as we drew up, as we walked towards our door. I waved at her and she smiled.

‘Take a break,’ said Dad. ‘You can finish the garden tomorrow. Go on. Go and see Mina.’

Fifteen

'The baby might not die,' I said.

'That's good,' said Mina.

I sat on the wall a few feet away from her.

'You weren't at school today,' she said.

'I wasn't well.'

She nodded.

'Not surprising, considering what you've been through.'

'You weren't at school, either,' I said.

'I don't go to school.'

I stared at her.

'My mother educates me,' she said. 'We believe that schools inhibit the natural curiosity, creativity and intelligence of children. The mind needs to be opened out into the world, not shuttered down inside a gloomy classroom.'

'Oh,' I said.

'Don't you agree, Michael?'

I thought of dashing across the yard with Leakey and Coot. I thought of Monkey Mitford's temper. I thought of Miss Clart's stories.

'Don't know,' I said.

'Our motto is on the wall by my bed,' she said. ' "How can a bird that is born for joy/Sit in a cage and sing?" William Blake.' She pointed up into the tree. 'The chicks in the nest won't need a classroom to make them fly. Will they?'

I shook my head.

'Well, then,' she said. 'My father believed this, too.'

'Your father?'

'Yes. He was a wonderful man. He died before I was born. We often think of him, watching us from Heaven.'

She watched me, with those eyes that seemed to get right inside.

'You're a quiet person,' she said.

I didn't know what to say. She began reading again.

'Do you believe we're descended from apes?' I said.

'Not a matter of belief,' she said. 'It's a proven fact. It's called evolution. You must know that. Yes, we are.'

She looked up from her book.

'I would hope, though,' she went on, 'that we also have some rather more beautiful ancestors. Don't you?'

She watched me again.

'Yes,' I said.

She read again. I watched the blackbird flying into the tree with worms drooping from its beak.

'It was great to see the owls,' I said.

She smiled.

'Yes. They're wild things, of course. Killers, savages. They're wonderful.'

'I kept dreaming I heard them, all through the night.'

'I listen for them, too. Sometimes in the dead of night when all the traffic's gone I hear them calling to each other.'

I joined my hands together tight with a space between my palms and a gap between my thumbs.

'Listen,' I said.

I blew softly into the gap and made the noise an owl makes.

'That's brilliant!' said Mina. 'Show me.'

I showed her how to put her hands together, how to blow. At first she couldn't do it, then she could. She hooted and grinned.

'Brilliant,' she said. 'So brilliant.'

'Leakey showed me,' I said. 'My mate at school.'

'I wonder if you did it at night if the owls would come.'

'Maybe. Maybe you should try it.'

'I will. Tonight I will.'

Hoot, she went. Hoot hoot hoot.

'Brilliant!' she said, and she clapped her hands.

'There's something I could show you as well,' I said. 'Like you showed me the owls.'

'What is it?'

'I don't know. I don't even know if it's true or if it's a dream.'

'That's all right. Truth and dreams are always getting muddled.'

'I'd have to take you there and show you.'

She opened her eyes wide and grinned, like she was ready to go right now.

'Can't go now,' I said.

Along the street, Dad opened the front door and waved.

'I've got to go,' I said. 'I've got to go and get 27 and 53.'

She raised her eyes.

'Mystery man,' she said. 'That's you.'

The blackbird flew out of the tree again.

I stood up to go.

I said, 'Do you know what shoulder blades are for?'

She giggled.

'Do you not even know that?' she said.

'Do you?'

'It's a proven fact, common knowledge. They're where your wings were, and where they'll grow again.'

She laughed again.

'Go on, then, mystery man. Go and get your mysterious numbers.'

Sixteen

Just before dawn, next morning.

I shone the torch on his white face.

'You again,' he squeaked.

'More 27 and 53,' I said.

'Food of the gods,' he said.

I squeezed through the tea chests to his side, held the tray for him and he hooked the food out with his finger. He slurped and licked and chewed.

'Nectar,' he whispered.

'How do you know about 27 and 53?' I said.

'Ernie's favourite. Used to hear him on the phone. 27 and 53, he used to say. Bring it round. Bring it quick.'

'You were in the house?'

'In the garden. Used to watch him through the windows. Used to listen to him. He was never very well. Couldn't eat it all. Used to find his leavings in the bin next morning. 27 and 53. Sweetest of nectars. Lovely change from spiders and mice.'

'Did he see you? Did he know you were there?'

'Never could tell. Used to look at me, but look right through me like I wasn't there. Miserable old toot. Maybe thought I was a figment.'

He dropped a long sticky string of pork and beansprouts on to his pale tongue.

He looked at me with his veiny eyes.

'You think I'm a figment?'

'Don't know what you are.'

'That's all right, then.'

'Are you dead?'

'Ha!'

'Are you?'

'Yes. The dead are often known to eat 27 and 53 and to suffer from Arthur Itis.'

'You need more aspirin?'

'Not yet.'

'Anything else?'

'27 and 53.'

He ran his finger around the tray and caught the final globs of sauce. He licked his pale lips with his pale tongue.

'The baby's in hospital,' I said.

'Some brown,' he said.

'Brown?'

'Brown ale. Something else Ernie used to have. Something else he couldn't finish. Eyes bigger than his belly. Something else I used to dig out of the bin, long as the bottle hadn't tipped over and spilt everything.'

'OK,' I said.

'Brown ale. Sweetest of nectars.'

He belched, retched, leaned forward. I shone the torch on to the great bulges on his back, beneath his jacket.

'There's someone I'd like to bring to see you,' I said when he'd settled.

'Someone to tell you I'm really here?'

'She's nice.'

'No.'

'She's clever.'

'Nobody.'

'She'll know how to help you.'

'Ha!'

He laughed but he didn't smile.

I didn't know why, but I started to tremble again.

He clicked his tongue and his breath rattled and sighed.

'I don't know what to do,' I said. 'The garage is going to bloody collapse. You're ill with bloody arthritis. You don't eat properly. I wake up and think of you and there's other things I need to think about. The baby's ill and we hope she won't die but she might. She really might.'

He tapped his fingers on the garage floor, ran his fingers through the furry balls that lay there.

'She's nice,' I told him. 'She'll tell nobody else. She's clever. She'll know how to help you.'

He shook his head.

'Damn kids,' he said.

'She's called Mina,' I said.

'Bring the street,' he said. 'Bring the whole damn town.'

'Just Mina. And me.'

'Kids.'

'What should I call you?'

'Eh?'

'What should I tell her you're called?'

'Nobody. Mr Nobody. Mr Bones and Mr Had Enough and Mr Arthur Itis. Now get out and leave me alone.'

'OK,' I said.

I stood up and started to back out between the tea chests.

I hesitated.

'Will you think about the baby?' I said.

'Eh?'

'Will you think about her in hospital? Will you think about her getting better?'

He clicked his tongue.

'Please,' I said.

'Yes. Blinking yes.'

I moved towards the door.

'Yes,' I heard him say again. 'Yes, I will.'

Outside, night had almost given way to day. The blackbird was on the garage roof, belting out its song. Black and pink and blue were mingling in the sky. I picked the cobwebs and bluebottles off myself. I heard the hooting as I turned back towards the house.

Hoot. Hoot hoot hoot.

I looked into the sky over the gardens and saw the owls heading homeward on great silent wings. I put my hands together and blew into the gap between my thumbs.

Hoot. Hoot hoot hoot.

Then I seemed to see a face, round and pale inside the darkness of an upstairs window in Mina's house. I put my hands together again.

Hoot. Hoot hoot hoot.

Something answered.

Hoot. Hoot hoot hoot.

Seventeen

At lunchtime I went to her front garden. She was sitting there on the lawn, on a spread-out blanket beneath the tree. She had her books, her pencils, her paints scattered around her. I was off school again. All morning I'd been clearing the wilderness again. Dad had been working in the front room, painting, stripping the walls, getting ready to hang wallpaper.

'The mystery man,' she said. 'Hello again.'

She had a book open at a skeleton of a bird. She'd been copying this into her sketch book.

'You're doing science?' I said.

She laughed.

'See how school shutters you,' she said. 'I'm drawing, painting, reading, looking. I'm feeling the sun and the air on my skin. I'm listening to the blackbird's song. I'm opening my mind. Ha! School!'

She picked up a book of poems from her blanket.

'Listen,' she said.

She sat up straight, coughed to clear her throat, held the opened book before her.

'To go to school in a summer morn,
O! it drives all joy away;
Under a cruel eye outworn,
The little ones spend the day
In sighing and dismay.'

She closed the book.

'William Blake again. You've heard of William Blake?'

'No.'

'He painted pictures and wrote poems. Much of the time he wore no clothes. He saw angels in his garden.'

She beckoned me. I stepped over the wall, sat on the blanket by her.

'Be quiet,' she whispered. 'Be very, very quiet. Listen.'

'Listen to what?'

'Just listen.'

I listened. I heard the traffic on Crow Road and the roads beyond. I heard birds singing. I heard the breeze in the trees. I heard my own breath.

'What can you hear?'

I told her.

'Listen deeper,' she said. 'Listen harder. Listen for the tiniest sweetest noise.'

I closed my eyes and listened again.

'What am I listening for?' I said.

'It comes from above you, from inside the tree.'

'Inside the tree?'

'Just do it, Michael.'

I tried to concentrate on the tree, on the branches and leaves, on the tiny shoots that grew out from the branches. I heard the shoots and leaves moving in the breeze.

'It comes from the nest,' she said. 'Just listen.'

I listened, and at last I heard it: a tiny squeaking sound, far-off, like it was coming from another world.

I caught my breath.

'Yes!' I whispered.

'The chicks,' she said.

Once I'd found it, and knew what it was and where it was, I could hear it along with all the other, stronger noises. I could open my eyes. I could look at Mina. Then I could close my eyes again and hear the blackbird chicks cheeping in the nest. I could imagine them there, packed close together in the nest.

'Their bones are more delicate than ours,' she said.

I opened my eyes. She was copying the skeleton again.

'Their bones are almost hollow. Did you know that?'

'Yes, I think so.'

She picked up a bone that was lying beside her books.

'This is from a pigeon, we believe,' she said. She snapped the bone and it splintered. She showed me that it wasn't solid inside, but was a mesh of needle-thin, bony struts.

'The presence of air cavities within the bone is known as pneumatisation,' she said. 'Feel it.'

I rested the bone on my palm. I looked at the spaces inside, felt the splinters.

'This too is the result of evolution,' she said. 'The bone is light but strong. It is adapted so that the bird can fly. Over millions of years, the bird has developed an anatomy that enables it to fly. As you know from the skeleton drawings you did the other day, we have not.'

She looked at me.

'You understand? You've covered this at school?'

'I think so.'

She watched me.

'One day I'll tell you about a being called the archaeopteryx,' she said. 'How's the baby today?'

'We'll see this afternoon. But I think she'll be OK.'

'Good.'

She put her hands together, blew between her thumbs, and made the owl sound.

'Brilliant!' she said. 'Brilliant!'

'I made the hooting noise last night,' I said. 'Just after dawn, very early in the morning.'

'Did you?'

'Were you looking out then? Did you make the hooting sound?'

'I can't be certain.'

'Can't?'

'I dream. I walk in my sleep. Sometimes I do things really and I think they were just dreams. Sometimes I dream them and think they were real.'

She stared at me.

'I dreamed about you last night,' she said.

'Did you?'

'Yes, but it's not important. You said you had a mystery. Something to show me.'

'I have.'

'Then show me.'

'Not now. This afternoon, maybe.'

She gazed into me.

'You were outside,' she said. 'There was an eerie light. You were very pale. There were cobwebs and flies all over you. You were hooting, just like an owl.'

We stared at each other.

Dad started calling.

'Michael! Michael!'

'See you later this afternoon,' I whispered.

Eighteen

'Mrs Dando was on the phone,' said Dad, on the way to the hospital. 'She was asking about you.'

'That's nice.'

'She said your mates want you back.'

'I'll see them Sunday.'

'Not missing school, then?'

I shrugged.

'Don't know.'

'Maybe you could go back soon, eh? Don't want to miss out on too much.'

'I learn a lot from Mina. She knows about lots of things, like birds and evolution.'

'Aye, there's that. And of course you've learned the Chinese menu off by heart.'

At the hospital the baby was still in the glass case, but the wires and tubes weren't in her. Mum lifted the lid back and I held the baby on my knee. I tried to feel if she was getting bigger and stronger. She squirmed, and I felt the long thin muscles in her back as she stretched. She took my finger in her fist and tried to squeeze it tight. She opened her eyes wide.

'Look,' said Dad. 'She's smiling at you.'

But it didn't seem like a smile to me.

A doctor came to see us. Doctor Bloom.

'She's coming on, then?' said Dad.

'Flying,' said the doctor.

'We'll have her back soon, then?'

Doctor Bloom shrugged. He touched the baby's cheek.

'We'll need to keep an eye on her,' he said. 'A few days, maybe.'

He smiled at me.

'Try not to worry, lad,' he said.

I touched the baby's shoulder blades, felt how tiny and flexible they were. I felt the thin rattle of her breath.

'She'll be running in the garden soon,' Mum said.

She laughed, but there were tears in her eyes.

She took the baby from me and rubbed cream on my skin again.

'You look tired,' she said. She looked at Dad. 'You two been staying up too late?'

'Dead right we have,' said Dad. 'It's been videos and Chinese takeaways all night, every night. Hasn't it, son?'

I nodded.

'Yes, it has.'

I went out into the corridor. I asked a nurse if she knew where the people with arthritis went. She said lots of them went to Ward 34 on the top floor. She said she thought that was a silly place to put people with bad bones who had such trouble walking and climbing stairs. I jumped into a lift and went up.

I stepped out of the lift and a woman came past me pushing a zimmer frame. She rested, puffing and grinning.

'Knackered,' she panted. 'Once up and down the ward and three times round the landing! Absolutely knackered!'

She leaned on the frame and looked me in the eye.

'But I'll be dancing soon.'

Her hands were twisted and her knuckles were swollen.

'Arthritis,' I said.

'That's right. Arthur. But I've got two new hips and I'll be dancing soon and that'll show him who's the boss. For a while at least.'

'I've got a friend with arthritis,' I said.

'Poor soul.'

'What'll help him?'

'Well, Arthur usually ends up winning in the end. But in the meantime some folk swear by cod liver oil and a positive mind. For me it's prayers to Our Lady, and Doctor MacNabola with his scissors and his saw and his plastic bits and pieces and his glue.'

She winked at me.

'Keep on moving. That's the thing. Keep the old bones moving. Don't let everything seize up.'

She shuffled on, humming 'Lord of the Dance'.

I followed the signs to Ward 34.

I looked inside. There were dozens of beds, facing each

other across the room. There were people practising moving on zimmer frames. Some lay in bed, smiling and knitting, wincing as they called across the ward to each other. Some lay exhausted, filled with pain. At the far end, a cluster of doctors and students in white coats gathered around a man in black. He spoke, and they scribbled in notebooks. He strode through the ward and they followed. He pointed at patients and they nodded and waved. He stopped at several of the beds and smiled for a moment as he listened to the patients. He shook hands with a nurse and headed quickly for the door. I stood there as the cluster approached me.

'Excuse me,' I said.

The man in black strode on.

'Doctor MacNabola,' I said.

He stopped and looked down at me. The doctors and students came to a halt around me.

'What's good for arthritis?' I said.

He blinked and grinned.

'The needle,' he said.

He pretended to squeeze a great syringe.

'Deep injections right into the joint.'

He winced, pretending to be in pain, and the doctors and students sniggered.

'Then the saw,' he said.

He made sawing movements with his arm and he gasped and twisted his face in agony.

'Bits cut out and new bits put in,' he said.

He pretended to thread a needle, then to sew.

'Stitch it up, good as new,' he said.

He sighed with relief, as if all his pain had gone.

He leaned towards me.

'Are you a sufferer, young man?'

I shook my head.

'A friend.'

The doctor stood up very straight.

'Then tell your friend to come to me. I'll needle him, saw him, fix him up and send him home nearly as good as new.'

The doctors sniggered again.

'Failing that,' he said, 'the advice is simple. Keep cheerful. Don't give up. Most of all, remain active. Take cod liver oil. Don't allow those joints to grind to a halt.'

He clasped his hands behind his back.

'Anything else?'

I shook my head.

He looked at the doctors around me.

'Any other advice for the young man's friend?'

They shook their heads.

'Then let us carry on,' he said, and he strode into the corridor.

I stood there thinking.

'You looking for someone?' said a nurse.

'No.'

She smiled.

'He's a good doctor, really,' she said. 'But he does like to show off. You tell your friend: keep moving, and try to smile. Don't make it easy for Arthur.'

I ran back to the lift and back to the baby's ward.

Mum and Dad were sitting holding hands, gazing down at the baby.

'Hello,' said Mum.

She tried to smile, but her voice was flat and I could see she'd been crying.

'Hello.'

'You've been a while.'

'All those Chinese takeaways,' said Dad, trying to get us to laugh.

'Cod liver oil,' she said. 'That'll sort you out.'

She held me tight.

'You're my best boy,' she whispered. 'Whatever happens, you'll always be my best boy.'

At home, as Dad prepared to get started again in the front room, I took a bottle of brown ale from the fridge and hid it with my torch just inside the garage door. I got my Swiss Army knife from my room. I took a handful of cod liver oil capsules from the bathroom and put them in my pocket.

I asked if it was OK if I went to see Mina again.

'Don't worry about me,' Dad said. 'I'll do all the dirty work. You just run around and have a good time.'

Nineteen

Her blanket and books were still on the lawn, but she wasn't there. I looked up into the tree and she wasn't there. I stepped over the wall, went to her front door, rang the doorbell. Her mother came.

'Is Mina in?' I asked.

She had jet-black hair like Mina's. She wore an apron covered in daubs of paint and clay.

'She is,' she said. She put her hand out. 'You must be Michael. I'm Mrs McKee.'

I shook her hand.

'Mina!' she shouted.

'How's the baby?' she asked.

'Very well. Well, we think she'll be very well.'

'Babies are stubborn things. Strugglers and fighters. Tell your parents I'm thinking of them.'

'I will.'

Mina came to the door. She had a paint-splashed apron on, too.

'We're modelling,' she said. 'Come and see.'

She led us through to the kitchen. There were big balls of clay in plastic bags on the table. The table was covered in a plastic sheet. There were knives and wooden tools. Mina's book of bird drawings was open at the blackbird. She showed me the clay she was working with. It was just a lump, but I could see the outline of a bird: a broad body, a pointed bill, a flattened tail. She added more clay and pinched the body and began to draw out its wings.

'Mina's fixated on birds just now,' said Mrs McKee. 'Sometimes it's things that swim, sometimes it's things that slink through the night, sometimes it's things that creep and crawl, but just now it's things that fly.'

I looked around. There was a shelf full of clay models: foxes, fish, lizards, hedgehogs, little mice. Then an owl, with its great round head, its pointed beak, its fierce claws.

'Did you make those?' I asked.

Mina laughed.

'They're brilliant,' I said.

She showed me how the clay would be shaped if the bird were in flight, how she could mark the feathers in with a pointed knife.

'Once it's fired and glazed I'll hang it from the ceiling.'

I picked up a piece of clay, rubbed it between my fingers, rolled it between my palms. It was cold and grainy. Mina licked her finger, rubbed the clay, showed how it could be made shiny smooth. I watched her, copied her. I worked the clay again, drew it into the shape of a snake, pushed it all together again and made the shape of a human head.

I thought of the baby. I started to shape her, her thin delicate form, her arms and legs, her head.

'Like magic, eh?' said Mina.

'Like magic, yes.'

'Sometimes I dream I make them so real they walk away or fly out of my hands. You use clay at school?'

'We do sometimes. We did in one class I was in.'

'Michael could come and work with us sometimes,' said Mina.

Mrs McKee looked at me. Her eyes were as piercing as Mina's, but more gentle.

'He could,' she said.

'I've told him what we think of schools,' said Mina.

Mrs McKee laughed.

'And I've told him about William Blake.'

I went on making the baby. I tried to form the features of her face. The clay started to dry out in the heat of my fingers. It started to crumble. I caught Mina's eye. I tried to tell her with my eyes that we had to go.

'Can I go for a walk with Michael?' she said immediately.

'Yes. Wrap your clay in plastic and you can get on with it when you come back.'

Twenty

I led her quickly along the front street, then I turned into the back lane. I led her past the high back garden walls.

'Where we going?' she said.

'Not far.'

I looked at her yellow top and blue jeans.

'The place is filthy,' I said. 'And it's dangerous.'

She buttoned the blouse to her throat. She clenched her fists.

'Good!' she said. 'Keep going, Michael!'

I opened our back garden gate.

'Here?' she said.

She stared at me.

'Yes. Yes!'

I stood at the garage door with her. She peered into the gloom. I picked up the beer and the torch.

'We'll need these,' I said. I took the capsules from my pocket. 'And these as well.'

Her eyes narrowed and she looked right into me.

'Trust me,' I said.

I hesitated.

'It's not just that it's dangerous,' I said. 'I'm worried that you won't see what I think I see.'

She took my hand and squeezed it.

'I'll see whatever's there,' she whispered. 'Take me in.'

I switched on the torch and stepped inside. Things scratched and scuttled across the floor. I felt Mina tremble. Her palms began to sweat.

I held her hand tight.

'It's all right,' I said. 'Just keep close to me.'

We squeezed between the rubbish and the broken furniture. Cobwebs snapped on our clothes and skin. Dead bluebottles attached themselves to us. The ceiling creaked and dust fell from the rotten timbers. As we approached the tea chests I started to shake. Maybe Mina would see nothing. Maybe I'd been wrong all along. Maybe dreams and truth were just a useless muddle in my mind.

I leaned forward, shone the light into the gap behind the tea chests.

'Again?' he squeaked.

I heard Mina stifle a cry. I felt her hand stiffen. I pulled her closer.

'It's all right,' I whispered.

'I brought my friend,' I said. 'Like I said I would. This is Mina.'

He turned his eyes towards her, then lowered them again.

I showed him the brown ale.

'I brought this as well.'

He laughed but he didn't smile.

I squeezed through to him. I snapped the cap off the bottle with the opener on the knife and crouched beside him. He tipped his head back and let me pour some of the beer into his mouth. He swallowed. Some of it trickled from his mouth on to his black suit.

'Nectar,' he sighed. 'Drink of the gods.'

He tipped his head back again, and I poured again.

I looked back at Mina's dark form looking down at us, her pale face, her mouth and eyes gaping in astonishment.

'Who are you?' she whispered.

'Mr Had Enough Of You,' he squeaked.

'I saw a doctor,' I said. 'Not Doctor Death. One that could fix you.'

'No doctors. Nobody. Nothing. Let me be.'

'You'll die. You'll crumble away and die.'

'Crumble crumble.' He tipped his head back. 'More beer.'

I poured more beer.

'I brought these as well,' I said.

I held a cod liver oil capsule out to him.

'Some people swear by them,' I said.

He sniffed.

'Stink of fish,' he squeaked. 'Slimy slithery swimming things.'

There were tears in my eyes.

'He just sits here,' I said. 'He doesn't care. It's like he's waiting to die. I don't know what to do.'

'Do nothing,' he squeaked.

He closed his eyes, lowered his head.

Mina came in beside us. She crouched, stared at his face as dry and pale as plaster, at the dead bluebottles and cobwebs, at the spiders and beetles that scuttled across him. She took the torch from me. She shone it on his thin body in the dark suit, on the long legs stretched out on the floor, on the swollen hands that rested at his side. She picked up one of the dark furry balls from beside him.

'Who are you?' she whispered.

'Nobody.'

She reached out and touched his cheek.

'Dry and cold,' she whispered. 'How long have you been here?'

'Long enough.'

'Are you dead?'

He groaned.

'Kids' questions. Always the same.'

'Tell her things,' I said. 'She's clever. She'll know what to do.'

He laughed but he didn't smile.

'Let me see her,' he said.

Mina turned the torch to her face, and it was brilliant white, with pitch dark gaps where her mouth and eyes were.

'I'm called Mina,' she said.

She sighed.

'I'm Mina,' she said. 'You're . . .?'

'You're Mina,' he said. 'I'm sick to death.'

She touched his hands. She lifted his filthy cuff and touched his scrawny twisted wrists.

'Calcification,' she said. 'The process by which the bone hardens, becomes inflexible. The process by which the body turns to stone.'

'Not as stupid as she looks,' he squeaked.

'It is linked to another process,' she said, 'by which the mind, too, becomes inflexible. It stops thinking and imagining. It becomes hard as bone. It is no longer a mind. It is a lump of bone wrapped in a wall of stone. This process is ossification.'

He sighed.

'More beer,' he said.

I poured more beer into his mouth.

'Take her away,' he whispered.

The roof trembled in the breeze. Dust fell on us.

Mina and I crouched close together, our knees almost resting on him. She twisted her face as she caught the stench of his breath. I took her hand and guided it to his shoulder blades. I pressed her fingertips against the bulge beneath his jacket. She leaned across him, felt his other shoulder blade. When she looked at me her eyes in the torchlight were shining bright.

Her face was almost touching his. Their pale skin bloomed in the torchlight.

'What are you?' she whispered.

No answer.

He sat there with his head lowered, his eyes closed.

'We can help you,' she whispered.

No answer.

I felt the tears running from my eyes.

'There's somewhere we could take you,' said Mina. 'It's safer there. Nobody would know. You could just sit there dying, too, if that's really what you want.'

Something brushed past us. I shone the torch down, saw Whisper entering the space behind the tea chests.

'Whisper!' said Mina.

The cat moved to his side, pressed itself against his damaged hands. He sighed.

'Smooth and soft,' he whispered.

His knuckles moved against the cat's soft fur.

'Sweet thing,' he whispered.

Whisper purred.

The timbers creaked. Dust fell on us again.

'Please let us take you somewhere else,' I said.

'More beer,' he whispered.

I held out a cod liver oil capsule.

'Take one of these as well,' I said.

He tipped his head back. I poured the beer in. I dropped the capsule on to his pale tongue.

He opened his eyes. He looked deep into Mina. She looked deep into him.

'You must let us help you,' she said.

He was silent for a long time.

'Do what you want,' he sighed.

Twenty-one

We stood in the wilderness. Whisper sat beneath us. We picked the bluebottles and webs out of each other's clothes and hair. Her eyes were burning bright.

'He's an extraordinary being,' she said.

The breeze blew and the garage creaked.

'We'll take him out tonight,' she said.

'At dawn,' I said.

'We'll call each other. We'll hoot like owls. We'll make sure we wake.'

We stared into each other.

'An extraordinary being,' she whispered.

She opened her hand and showed me the dark ball of congealed skin and bone she had brought out with her.

'What is it?' I said.

She bit her lip.

'It can't be what I think it is,' she said. 'It can't be.'

Dad came to the back window. He stood there watching us.

'I'll go back now,' I said. 'I'll carry on doing the garden.'

'I'll go back to making the blackbird.'

'I'll see you at dawn.'

'At dawn. I won't sleep.'

She squeezed my hand, slipped out through the gate with Whisper at her heels.

I turned back into the wilderness. I waved at Dad. My heart was thundering. I knelt in the soil, wrenched at the weeds, sent black beetles scattering.

'He won't die,' I whispered. 'He won't just die.'

Later, Dad came out. We drank orange juice together and sat against the house wall.

He grinned.

'You like Mina, then,' he said.

I shrugged.

'You do,' he said.

'She's extraordinary,' I said.

Twenty-two

I was with the baby. We were tucked up together in the blackbird's nest. Her body was covered in feathers and she was soft and warm. The blackbird was on the house roof, flapping its wings, squawking. Doctor MacNabola and Doctor Death were beneath us in the garden. They had a table filled with knives and scissors and saws. Doctor Death had a great syringe in his fist.

'Bring her down!' he yelled. 'We'll make her good as new!'

The baby squeaked and squealed in fright. She stood at the edge of the nest, flapping her wings, trying for the first time to fly. I saw the great bare patches on her skin: she didn't have enough feathers yet, her wings weren't strong enough yet. I tried to reach for her but my arms were hard and stiff as stone.

'Go on!' the doctors yelled. They laughed. 'Go on, baby! Fly!'

Doctor MacNabola lifted a shining saw.

She teetered on the brink.

Then I heard the hooting of an owl. I opened my eyes. Pale light was glowing at my window. I looked down, saw Mina in the wilderness with her hands against her face.

Hoot. Hoot hoot hoot.

'I didn't sleep all night,' I said, once I'd tiptoed out to her. 'Then at the very last minute when the night was ending I did.'

'But you're awake now?' she said.

'Yes.'

'We're not dreaming this?'

'We're not dreaming it.'

'We're not dreaming it together?'

'Even if we were we wouldn't know.'

The blackbird flew to the garage roof, began its morning song.

'No time to waste,' I said.

We went to the door, stepped inside. We moved swiftly through the furniture. I shone the torch on his face.

'You have to come with us,' said Mina.

He sighed, groaned.

'I'm ill,' he said.

He didn't look at us.

'I'm sick to death,' he said.

We squeezed through the gap between the tea chests and crouched before him.

'You have to come,' she said again.

'I'm weak as a baby,' he said.

'Babies aren't weak,' she whispered. 'Have you seen a baby

screaming for its food or struggling to crawl? Have you seen a blackbird chick daring its first flight?'

She put her hand beneath his armpit. She tugged at him.

'Please,' she whispered.

I held him, too. I tugged. We felt him beginning to relax, to give himself up to us.

'I'm frightened,' he squeaked.

Mina bent close to him. She kissed his pale cheek.

'Don't be frightened. We're taking you to safety.'

His joints creaked as he struggled to rise from the floor. He whimpered in pain. He leaned against us. He tottered and wobbled as he rose. He was taller than us, tall as Dad. We felt how thin he was, how extraordinarily light he was. We had our arms around him. Our fingers touched behind his back. We explored the growths upon his shoulder blades. We felt them folded up like arms. We felt their soft coverings. We stared into each other's eyes and didn't dare to tell each other what we thought we felt.

'Extraordinary, extraordinary being,' whispered Mina.

'Can you walk?' I said.

He whimpered, squeaked.

'Move slowly,' I said. 'Hold on to us.'

I moved backwards, between the tea chests. Mina supported him from behind. His feet dragged across the ruined floor. Things scuttled across us. The garage creaked. Dust fell. His breathing was hoarse, uneven. His body shuddered. He whimpered with pain. At the door he closed his eyes, turned his head away from the intensifying light. Then he turned again and faced the daylight. Through narrowed veiny eyes he looked out through the door. Mina and I gazed at his face, so pale and plaster dry. His skin was cracked and crazed. His black hair was a tangle of knots. Dust, cobwebs, bluebottles, spiders, beetles clung to him and fell from him. We saw for the first time that he wasn't old. He seemed like a young man. Mina whispered it:

'You're beautiful!'

I peeped out across the wilderness towards the house, saw nobody at the window.

'Keep moving.'

I opened the gate, drew him by the hand. He leaned on Mina, shuffled out after me into the lane.

I closed the gate.

Already traffic could be heard in the city, on nearby Crimdon Road. The birds in the gardens and on the rooftops yelled their songs. Whisper appeared at our side.

'We'll carry him,' I said.

'Yes,' said Mina.

I stood behind him and he leaned back into my arms. Mina took his feet.

We caught our breath at our ability to do this thing, at the extraordinary lightness of our load. I closed my eyes for a moment. I imagined that this was a dream. I told myself that anything was possible in a dream. I felt the great bulges at his back bundled up against my arms. We started to move.

We walked through the back lane, turned into another back lane, hurried to the green gate of the boarded house.

Mina opened it with her key. We went through. We hurried to the door with the red sign: DANGER. Mina opened it with her key. We moved through into the darkness, then into the first room and we laid him on the floor.

We trembled and gasped. He whimpered with pain. We touched him gently.

'You're safe,' said Mina.

She took off her cardigan. She folded it and lay it beneath his head.

'We'll bring you more things to make you comfortable,' she said.

'We'll make you well. Is there anything you would like?'

I smiled.

'27 and 53,' I said.

'27 and 53,' he whimpered.

'I'll have to go back,' I said. 'My Dad'll wake up soon.'

'Me, too,' said Mina.

We smiled at each other. We looked at him, lying beside us.

'We won't be long,' I said.

Mina kissed his pale cracked cheek. She stretched her arms once more around his back. Her eyes burned with astonishment and joy.

'Who are you?' she whispered.

He winced with pain.

'My name is Skellig,' he said.

Twenty-three

Mrs Dando called that morning just after breakfast. She came on her bike on her way to school. She said my mates were looking forward to getting me back again.

'They say you're the best tackler in the school,' she said.

Dad showed her all the work we'd done on the house. We showed her the wilderness. She said everything would be bright and new for when the baby came home. She took her bag off her back. She took out a little cuddly black bear for Dad to give to the baby.

'And there's this for you,' she laughed. 'Sorry!'

It was a folder of homework from Rasputin and Monkey: worksheets with gaps to fill in and questions to answer. There was a note from Miss Clarts: No real homework. Write a story. Get well soon! There were sheets of maths problems and a book called *Julius And The Wilderness* with a red sticker on the back.

Dad laughed as we watched her cycle away.

'No rest for the wicked, eh, son?' he said. 'I'll do the decorating. You get on with your work.'

I got a biro and took the work along the street to Mina's front garden. She was sitting with her mum on the blanket underneath the tree. Her mum was reading, Mina was scribbling fast in a black book. She grinned, and beckoned me over the wall when she saw me standing there.

Mina looked at the worksheets.

It is thought that Man is d________ from the apes.

This is the Theory of E________.

This theory was developed by Charles D________.

There was sentence after sentence like that.

Mina read the sentences out loud.

She said, 'Blank blank blank,' in a singsong voice when she came to the dashes.

She stopped after the first three sentences and just looked at me.

'Is this really the kind of thing you do all day?' she said.

'Mina,' said her mum.

Mina giggled. She flicked through the book. It was about a boy who tells magical tales that turn out to be true.

'Yeah, looks good,' she said. 'But what's the red sticker for?'

'It's for confident readers,' I said. 'It's to do with reading age.'

'And what if other readers want to read it?'

'Mina,' said her mum.

'And where would William Blake fit in?' said Mina. ' "Tyger! Tyger! burning bright/In the forests of the night".

Is that for the best readers or the worst readers? Does that need a good reading age?'

I stared back at her. I didn't know what to say. I wanted to get back over the wall and go home again.

'And if it was for the worst readers would the best readers not bother with it because it would be too stupid for them?' she said.

'Mina,' said her mum. She was smiling gently at me. 'Take no notice,' she said. 'She's a madam sometimes.'

'Well,' said Mina.

She went back to scribbling in the black book again.

She looked up at me.

'Go on, then,' she said. 'Do your homework, like a good schoolboy.'

Her mum smiled again.

'I'll get on inside,' she said. 'You tell her to shut up if she starts getting at you again. OK?'

'OK,' I said.

After she'd gone we said nothing for ages. I pretended to read *Julius And The Wilderness*, but it was like the words were dead and meaningless.

'What you writing?' I said at last.

'My diary. About me and you and Skellig,' she said.

She didn't look up.

'What if somebody reads it?' I said.

'Why would they read it? They know it's mine and it's private.'

She scribbled again.

I thought about our diaries at school. We filled them in every week. Every so often, Miss Clarts checked that they were neat and the punctuation was right and the spellings were right. She gave us marks for them, just like we got marks for attendance and punctuality and attitude and everything else we did. I said nothing about this to Mina. I went on pretending to read the book. I felt tears in my eyes. That made me think about the baby and doing that just made the tears worse.

'I'm sorry,' said Mina. 'I really am. One of the things we hate about schools is the sarcasm that's in them. And I'm being sarcastic.'

She squeezed my hand.

'It's so exciting,' she whispered. 'You, me, Skellig. We'll have to go to him. He'll be waiting for us. What shall we take for him?'

Twenty-four

'What is this place?' I asked her as she opened the gate and we stepped into the long back garden.

We ducked down and hurried to the DANGER door.

'It was my grandfather's,' she said. 'He died last year. He left it to me in his will. It'll be mine when I'm eighteen.' She turned the key in the lock. 'We're having it repaired soon. Then we'll rent it out.'

We stepped inside, carrying our parcels. Whisper slipped in at our heels.

'Don't worry, though,' she whispered. 'There's weeks before the builders come.'

I switched my torch on. We went into the room where we'd left him. He wasn't there. The room was silent and empty, as if he'd never been there at all. Then we saw Mina's cardigan behind the door, and dead bluebottles on the floor-boards, and heard Whisper mewing from the stairs. We went into the hallway, saw the shape of Skellig lying halfway up the first flight.

'Knackered,' he squeaked as we crouched beside him.

'Sick to death. Aspirin.'

I fiddled in his pocket, took two of the tablets out, popped them in his mouth.

'You moved,' I said. 'All on your own, you moved.'

He winced with pain.

'You want to go higher,' said Mina.

'Yes. Somewhere higher,' he whispered.

We left our parcels there, lifted him together and carried him to the first landing.

He groaned and twisted in agony.

'Put me down,' he squeaked.

We took him into a bedroom with high white ceilings and pale wallpapered walls. We rested him against the wall. Thin beams of light pierced the cracks in the boards on the windows and shone on to his pale, dry face.

I hurried back down for the parcels. We unrolled the blankets we had brought. We laid them out with a pillow on the floor. We put down a little plastic dish for his aspirins and cod liver oil. I put an opened bottle of beer beside it. There was a cheese sandwich and half a bar of chocolate.

'All for you,' Mina whispered.

'Let us help you,' I said.

He shook his head. He turned over, on to all fours, started to crawl the short distance towards the blankets. We saw his tears dropping through the beams of light, splashing on to the floor. He knelt by the blankets, panting. Mina went to him, knelt facing him.

'I'll make you more comfortable,' she whispered.

She unfastened the buttons on his jacket. She began to pull his jacket down over his shoulders.

'No,' he squeaked.

'Trust me,' she whispered.

He didn't move. She slid the sleeves down over his arms, took the jacket right off him. We saw what both of us had dreamed we might see. Beneath his jacket were wings that grew out through rips in his shirt. When they were released, the wings began to unfurl from his shoulder blades. They were twisted and uneven, they were covered in cracked and crooked feathers. They clicked and trembled as they opened. They were wider than his shoulders, higher than his head. Skellig hung his head towards the floor. His tears continued to fall. He whimpered with pain. Mina reached out to him, stroked his brow. She reached further and touched the feathers with her fingertips.

'You're beautiful,' she whispered.

'Let me sleep,' squeaked Skellig. 'Let me go home.'

He lay face down and his wings continued to quiver into shape above him. We drew the blankets up beneath them, felt his feathers against the skin on the backs of our hands. Soon Skellig's breathing settled and he slept. Whisper rested against him, purring.

We stared at each other. My hand trembled as I reached out towards Skellig's wings. I touched them with my fingertips. I rested my palms on them. I felt the feathers, and beneath them the bones and sinews and muscles that supported them. I felt the crackle of Skellig's breathing.

I tiptoed to the shutters and stared out through the narrow chinks.

'What you doing?' she whispered.

'Making sure the world's still really there,' I said.

Twenty-five

The wires and the tubes were in her again. The glass case was shut. She didn't move. She was wrapped in white. Her hair was fluffy, dead straight and dark. I wanted to touch it, and to touch her skin, feel it soft against my fingertips. Her little hands were clenched tight on either side of her head. We said nothing. I listened to the drone of the city outside, to the clatter of the hospital. I heard my own breathing, the scared quick breathing of my parents at my side. I heard them sniffing back their tears. I went on listening. I listened through all these noises, until I heard the baby, the gentle squeaking of her breath, tiny and distant as if it came from a different world. I closed my eyes and went on listening and listening. I listened deeper, until I believed I heard her beating heart. I told myself that if I listened hard enough her breathing and the beating of her heart would never be able to stop.

Dad held my hand as we walked through the corridors towards the car park. We passed a lift shaft and the woman with the zimmer frame from upstairs tottered out. She gasped and rested on her frame and grinned at me.

'Three times round every landing and three times up and down in the lift,' she said. 'Knackered. Absolutely knackered.'

Dad blinked, and nodded kindly at her.

'Blinking getting there!' she said. She bobbed about inside the frame. 'Be dancing soon, you see!'

She patted my arm with her crooked hand.

'You're so sad today. Been to see that friend of yours?'

I nodded, and she smiled.

'I'm going home soon. He will, too. Keep moving, that's the thing. Stay cheerful.'

She hobbled away, singing 'Lord of the Dance' to herself.

'Who did she mean, your friend?' said Dad.

'Nobody.'

He was too distracted to ask again.

In the car I saw the tears running down his face.

I closed my eyes. I remembered the sound of the baby's breathing, her beating heart. I held them in my mind, went on listening to them. I touched my heart and I felt the baby's heart beating beside my own. Traffic roared past, Dad sniffed back his tears. I stayed dead silent, and concentrated on keeping the baby safe.

Twenty-six

'There it is,' said Mina. 'Archaeopteryx. The dinosaur that flew.'

She laid the heavy encyclopedia on the grass beneath the tree. We looked down at the clumsy creature. It was perched on a thorny branch. Beyond it, volcanoes belched flames and smoke. The great land-bound creatures – diplodocus, stegosaurus – lurched across a stony plain.

'We believe that dinosaurs became extinct,' said Mina. 'But there's another theory, that their descendants are with us still. They nest in our trees and our attics. The air is filled with their songs. The little archaeopteryx survived, and began the line of evolution that led to birds.'

She touched the short, stunted wings.

'Wings and feathers, see? But the creature was a heavy, bony thing. Look at the clumsy, leaden tail. It was capable of nothing but short, sudden flights. From tree to tree, stone to stone. It couldn't rise and spiral and dance like birds can now. No pneumatisation.'

I looked at her.

'Do you remember nothing?' she said. 'Pneumatisation. The presence of air cavities in the bones of birds. It is this which allows them free flight.'

The blackbird flew from the tree above us and dashed into the sky.

'If you held the archaeopteryx,' she said, 'it would be almost as heavy as stone in your hand. It would be almost as heavy as the clay models I make.'

I looked into Mina's dark eyes. They were wide open, expectant, like she wanted me to see something or say something. I thought of the baby in my lap, of Skellig slung between Mina and me. I thought of his wings and of the baby's fluttering heart.

'There's no end to evolution,' said Mina.

She shuffled closer to me.

'We have to be ready to move forward,' she said. 'Maybe this is not how we are meant to be for ever.'

She took my hand.

'We are extraordinary,' she whispered.

She looked deep into me.

'Skellig!' she whispered. 'Skellig! Skellig!'

I stared back. I didn't blink. It was like she was calling Skellig out from somewhere deep inside me. It was like we were looking into the place where each other's dreams came from.

And then there was sniggering and giggling. We looked up, and there were Leakey and Coot, standing on the other side of the wall, looking down at us.

Twenty-seven

'What's wrong with you?' they kept asking. 'What's bloody wrong with you?'

I was hopeless. I couldn't tackle. I missed the ball by a mile when I jumped up to head it. When I had the ball at my feet I stumbled all over the place. I fell over it once and skinned my elbow on the kerb. I felt shaky and wobbly and I didn't want to be doing this, playing football in our front street with Leakey and Coot while Mina sat in the tree with a book in her lap and stared and stared.

'It's cos he's been ill,' said Leakey.

'Bollocks,' said Coot. 'He's not been ill. He's just been upset.'

He watched me trying to flick the ball up on to my head. It bounced off my knee and bobbed into the gutter.

'I'm just out of practice,' I said.

'Bollocks,' he said. 'It's just been a week since you could beat anybody in the school.'

'That's right,' said Leakey.

'It's her,' said Coot. 'Her in the tree. That lass he was with.'

Leakey grinned.

'That's right,' he said.

I shook my head.

'Bollocks,' I whispered.

My voice was as shaky as my feet had been.

They stood there sniggering.

'It's that lass,' said Leakey.

'That lass that climbs in a tree like a monkey,' said Coot. 'Her that sits in a tree like a crow.'

'Bollocks,' I said.

I looked Leakey in the eye. He'd been my best friend for years. I couldn't believe he'd go on with this if I looked him in the eye and wanted him to stop.

He grinned.

'He holds hands with her,' he said.

'She says he's extraordinary,' said Coot.

'Get stuffed,' I said.

I turned away from them, went past our house to the end of the street, turned down towards the back lane. I heard them coming after me. I sat down in the lane with my back against the boarded-up garage. I just wanted them to go away. I wanted them to stay. I wanted to be able to play like I used to. I wanted things to be just the way they used to be.

Leakey crouched beside me and I could feel he was sorry.

'The baby's ill,' I said. 'Really ill. The doctor says I'm in distress.'

'Yeah,' he said. 'Yeah. I know. I'm sorry.'

Coot kicked the ball back and forward against the boards.

'Don't do that,' I said. 'You'll knock it down.'

He sniggered.

'Oh, aye?'

He went on doing it.

'Don't do it,' I said.

I got up and grabbed him by the scruff of the neck.

'Stop doing it,' I said.

He sniggered again.

'Doing what, Michael?' he said in a high girlish voice.

I shoved him back against the garage. I thumped my hand against the boards beside his head.

He winked at Leakey.

'See what I mean?' he said.

I thumped the boards beside his head again. There was a loud crack and the whole garage trembled. Coot jumped away. We stared at the boards.

'Bloody hell,' said Leakey.

There was another crack and another shudder and then silence.

I opened the gate into the wilderness and we tiptoed inside. We stared through the door into the gloomy garage. Dust was falling thicker than ever through the light.

There was another crack.

'Bloody hell,' said Coot.

'I'd better get my dad,' I said.

Twenty-eight

Very gently, using a little hammer and long thin nails, he nailed some boards across the door. The garage trembled as he worked. He told us to keep back. We stood in the wilderness staring, shaking our heads. He got some black gloss paint and wrote DANGER across the boards. He brought some Coke for us and some beer for himself and we all sat against the house wall and stared at the garage.

'Better get it made safe, eh?' said Dad.

'My uncle's a builder,' said Coot. 'Always doing garages and extensions and things.'

'Aye?' said Dad.

'He'd tell you knock the whole thing down and start again.'

'Aye?'

'Aye. Some folk fight to keep things that should've been smashed years back.'

I looked at the garage and imagined it gone, saw the big emptiness that would take its place.

'Aye,' said Coot again. 'He says the best jobs start with a

massive sledgehammer and a massive skip.'

He swigged his Coke. The blackbird flew on to the edge of the garage roof and perched there. I knew it would be watching the wilderness, looking for beetles and fat worms for its babies.

'He wants us gone,' I said.

Coot cocked his finger and thumb like a gun. He eyed the bird as if he was aiming.

'Gotcha,' he said, and his hand recoiled as if he'd fired.

Dad told Leakey and Coot it was good to see them again.

'Michael's been moping,' he said. 'A good kickabout with his mates'll be just what the doctor ordered.'

'Not against the garage, though,' said Leakey.

'Not against the blinking garage, no.'

We took the ball and went through the house into the front street again. Mina wasn't there. I played better now, but I couldn't help turning to the empty tree. I imagined her alone with Skellig in the dark house.

I caught them laughing at me.

'Missing her already?' said Coot.

I raised my eyes and tried to grin. I went to sit on our front garden wall.

'Who is she, anyway?' said Leakey.

I shrugged.

'She's called Mina.'

'What school's she at?'

'She doesn't go to school.'

They looked at me.

'How's that?' said Leakey.

'Plays the wag?' said Coot.

'Her mother teaches her,' I said.

They looked again.

'Bloody hell,' said Leakey. 'I thought you had to go to school.'

'Imagine it,' said Coot.

They imagined it for a while.

'Lucky sod,' said Leakey.

'What'll she do for mates, though?' said Coot. 'And who'd like to be stuck at home all day?'

'They think schools stop you from learning,' I said. 'They think schools try to make everybody just the same.'

'That's bollocks,' said Coot.

'Aye,' said Leakey. 'You're learning all day long in school.'

I shrugged.

'Maybe.'

'Is that why you've not been coming in?' said Leakey. 'Is it cos you're never coming back again. You're going to let that lass's mother teach you?'

'Course not,' I said. 'But they're going to teach me some things.'

'Like?'

'Like modelling with clay. And about William Blake.'

'Who's he?' said Coot. 'That bloke that's got the butcher's shop in town?'

'He said school drives all joy away,' I said. 'He was a painter and a poet.'

They looked at each other and grinned. Leakey couldn't look me in the eye. I could feel my face burning and burning.

'Look,' I said. 'I can't tell you anything. But the world's full of amazing things.'

Coot sighed and shook his head and bounced the ball between his knees.

'I've seen them,' I said.

Leakey stared at me.

I imagined taking him through the DANGER door, taking him to Skellig, showing him. For a moment I was dying to tell him what I'd seen and what I'd touched.

'There she is,' said Coot.

We turned together, and there was Mina climbing into the tree again.

'The monkey girl,' said Leakey.

Coot giggled.

'Hey!' he said. 'Maybe Rasputin's right about that evolution stuff. He could come and look at her and see there's monkeys all around us still.'

Twenty-nine

Her eyes were cold as she stared down at me from the tree. Her voice was sarcastic and singsong:

> 'Thank God I was never sent to school,
> To be flogd into following the style of a Fool.'

'You know nothing about it,' I said. 'We don't get flogged and my friends aren't fools.'

'Ha!'

'That's it,' I said. 'You know nothing about it. You think you're special but you're just as ignorant as anybody. You might know about William Blake but you know nothing about what ordinary people do.'

'Ha!'

'Yes. Ha!'

I stared at my feet. I picked my fingernails. I kicked the garden wall.

'They hate me,' she said. 'I could see it in their eyes. They think I'm taking you away from them. They're stupid.'

'They're not stupid!'

'Stupid. Kicking balls and jumping at each other and screeching like hyenas. Stupid. Yes, hyenas. You as well.'

'Hyenas? They think you're a monkey, then.'

Her eyes glared and her face burned.

'See? See what I mean? They know nothing about me but they hate me.'

'And of course you know everything about them.'

'I know enough. There's nothing to know. Kicking, screeching, being stupid.'

'Ha!'

'Yes, ha! And that little ginger one . . .'

'Blake was little and ginger.'

'How do you know that?'

'See? You think nobody but you can know anything!'

'No, I don't!'

'Ha!'

Her lips were pressed tight together. She pressed her head back against the trunk of the tree.

'Go home,' she said. 'Go and play stupid football or something. Leave me alone.'

I gave the wall a last kick, then I left her. I went into my front garden. I went through the open front door. Dad shouted hello from somewhere upstairs. I went straight through into the wilderness and squatted there and squeezed my eyes tight to try and stop the tears.

Thirty

The owls woke me. Or a call that was like that of the owls. I looked out into the night. The moon hung over the city, a great orange ball with the silhouettes of steeples and chimney stacks upon it. The sky was blue around it, deepening to blackness high above, where only the most brilliant stars shone. Down below, the wilderness was filled with the pitch black shadow of the garage and a wedge of cold silvery light.

I watched for the birds and saw nothing.

'Skellig,' I whispered. 'Skellig. Skellig.'

I cursed myself, because in order to go to him now I had to rely on Mina.

I lay in bed again. I moved between sleeping and waking. I dreamt that Skellig entered the hospital ward, that he lifted the baby from her glass case. He pulled the tubes and wires from her. She reached up and touched his pale, dry skin with her little fingers and she giggled. He took her away, flew with her in his arms through the darkest part of the sky. He landed with her in the wilderness and stood there calling to me.

'Michael! Michael!'

They stood there laughing. She bounced in his arms. They had lost all of their weaknesses and they were strong again.

'Michael!' he called, and his eyes were shining with joy. 'Michael! Michael! Michael!'

I woke up. I heard the owls again. I pulled on some jeans and a pullover and tiptoed downstairs and out into the wilderness. Nothing there, of course, just the image of them burning in my mind. I stood listening to the city all around, its low, deep, endless roar. I went out through the shadows into the back lane. Though I knew it was useless, I began to walk towards Mina's boarded house. Something brushed against me as I walked.

'Whisper!' I whispered.

The cat went with me, slinking at my side.

The door into the garden was ajar. The moon had climbed. It hung directly over us. Behind the wall, the garden was flooded with its light. Mina was waiting. She sat on the step before the DANGER door, elbows resting on her knees, pale face resting on her hands. I hesitated and we watched each other.

'What took so long?' she said.

I looked at her.

'Thought I'd have to do this all alone,' she said.

'Thought that was what you wanted.'

The cat prowled to her side, brushed itself against her legs.

'Oh, Michael,' she said.

I didn't know what to do. I sat on the steps below her.

'We said stupid things,' she said. 'I said stupid things.'

I said nothing. An owl silently flew down into the garden and perched on the back wall.

Hoot, it went. Hoot hoot hoot.

'Don't be angry. Be my friend,' she whispered.

'I am your friend.'

'It's possible to hate your friend. You hated me today.'

'You hated me.'

The other owl descended and perched in silence beside its partner.

'I love the night,' said Mina. 'Anything seems possible at night when the rest of the world has gone to sleep.'

I looked up at her silvery face, her ink-black eyes. I knew that in a dream I would see her as the moon with Skellig flying silently across her.

I moved up to her side.

'I'll be your friend,' I whispered.

She smiled, and we sat there looking out at the moonlight. Soon the owls rose, and headed for the centre of the city. We lay back together against the DANGER door. I felt myself falling into sleep.

'Skellig!' I hissed. 'Skellig!'

We rubbed the sleep from our eyes.

Mina pushed the key into the lock.

Thirty-one

We had no torch. The light that came through the chinks in the boards was pale and weak. We blundered through the dark. We held hands and stretched our free hands out in front of us. We walked into the wall. We caught our toes on loose floorboards. We stumbled as we climbed the stairs. We shuffled across the first landing. We felt for the handle of the door to the room where we thought we'd left Skellig. We inched the door open. We whispered, 'Skellig! Skellig!' No answer. We moved forward carefully, arms outstretched, feeling forward with our feet before we took each step. Our breath was fast, shallow, trembly. My heart was thundering. I opened my eyes wide, glared into the dark, seeking the shape of his body on the floor. Nothing there, just the blankets, the pillow, the plastic dish, the beer bottle rolling away from my stumbling feet.

'Where is he?' whispered Mina.

'Skellig,' we whispered. 'Skellig! Skellig!'

We turned back to the landing again, we stumbled up the next flight of stairs, we opened many doors, we stared past them into pitch black rooms, we whispered his name, we heard nothing but our own breath, our own uncertain feet, his name echoing back to us from bare floorboards and bare walls, we turned back to the landing again, we stumbled up the next flight of stairs.

We halted. We gripped each other's hand. We felt each other shuddering. Our heads were filled with the darkness of the house. Beside me was nothing but Mina's face, its silvery bloom.

'We must be more calm,' she whispered. 'We must listen, like we listened to the squeaking of the blackbird chicks.'

'Yes,' I said.

'Stand still. Do nothing. Listen to the deepest deepest places of the dark.'

We held hands and listened to the night. We heard the endless din of the city all around us, the creaking and cracking of the house, our own breath. As I listened deeper, I heard the breathing of the baby deep inside myself. I heard the far-off beating of her heart. I sighed, knowing that she was safe.

'You hear?' said Mina.

I listened, and it was as if she guided me to hear what she heard. It was like hearing the blackbird chicks cheeping in the nest. It came from above us, a far-off squeaking, whistling sound. Skellig's breathing.

'I hear it,' I whispered.

We climbed the final flight of stairs towards the final doorway. Gently, fearfully, we turned the handle and slowly pushed open the door.

Moonlight came through the arched window. Skellig sat before its frame, bowed forward. We saw the black silhouette of his pale face, of his bowed shoulders, of his wings folded upon his shoulders. At the base of his wings was the silhouette of his shredded shirt. He must have heard us as we stepped through the door, as we crouched together against the wall, but he didn't turn. We didn't speak. We didn't dare approach him. As we watched, an owl appeared, dropping on silent wings from the moonlit sky to the moonlit window. It perched on the frame. It bowed forward, opened its beak, laid something on the windowsill and flew out again. Skellig bent his head to where the bird had been. He pressed his lips to the windowsill. Then the owl, or the other owl, came again to the window, perched, opened its beak, flew off again. Skellig bent forward again. He chewed.

'They're feeding him,' whispered Mina.

And it was true. Each time the owls left, Skellig lifted what they had left him, he chewed and swallowed.

At last he turned to us. We saw nothing of his eyes, his pale cheeks; just his black silhouette against the glistening night. Mina and I held hands. Still we didn't dare go to him.

'Come to me,' he whispered.

We didn't move.

'Come to me.'

Mina tugged me, led me to him.

We met him in the middle of the room. He stood erect. He seemed stronger than he'd ever been. He took my hand and Mina's hand, and we stood there, the three of us, linked in the moonlight on the old bare floorboards. He squeezed my hand as if to reassure me. When he smiled at me I caught the stench of his breath, the stench of the things the owls had given him to eat. I gagged. His breath was the breath of an animal that lives on the meat of other living things: a dog, a fox, a blackbird, an owl. He squeezed me again and smiled again. He stepped sideways and we turned together, kept slowly turning, as if we were carefully, nervously beginning to dance. The moonlight shone on our faces in turn. Each face spun from shadow to light, from shadow to light, from shadow to light, and each time the faces of Mina and Skellig came into the light they were more silvery, more expressionless. Their eyes were darker, more empty, more penetrating. For a moment I wanted to pull away from them, to break the circle, but Skellig's hand tightened on mine.

'Don't stop, Michael,' he whispered.

His eyes and Mina's eyes stared far into me.

'No, Michael,' said Mina. 'Don't stop.'

I didn't stop. I found that I was smiling, that Skellig and Mina were smiling too. My heart raced and thundered and then it settled to a steady rolling rhythm. I felt Skellig's and Mina's hearts beating along with my own. I felt their breath in rhythm with mine. It was like we had moved into each other, as if we had become one thing. Our heads were dark, then were as huge and moonlit as the night. I couldn't feel the bare floorboards against my feet. All I knew were the hands in mine, the faces turning through the light and the dark, and for a moment I saw ghostly wings at Mina's back,

I felt the feathers and delicate bones rising from my own shoulders, and I was lifted from the floor with Skellig and Mina. We turned circles together through the empty air of that empty room high in an old house in Crow Road.

Then it was over. I found myself crumpled on the floorboards alongside Mina. Skellig crouched beside us. He touched our heads.

'Go home now,' he squeaked.

'But how are you like this now?' I asked.

He pressed his finger to his lips.

'The owls and the angels,' he whispered.

He raised his finger when we began to speak again.

'Remember this night,' he whispered.

We tottered from the room. We descended the stairs. We went out through the DANGER door into the night. We hesitated for a moment.

'Did it happen to you as well?' I whispered.

'Yes. It happened to all of us.'

We laughed. I closed my eyes. I tried to feel again the feathers and bones of wings on my shoulders. I opened my eyes, tried to recall the ghostly wings rising at Mina's back.

'It will happen again,' said Mina. 'Won't it?'

'Yes.'

We hurried homeward. At the entrance to the back lane, we paused again to catch our breath. It was then that we heard Dad's voice, calling.

'Michael! Michael!'

As we stood there, we saw him come out from the

wilderness into the lane. His voice was filled with fear.

'Michael! Oh, Michael!'

Then he saw us standing there, hand in hand.

'Michael! Oh, Michael!'

He ran and grabbed me in his arms.

'We were sleepwalking,' said Mina.

'Yes,' I said, as he held me tight to keep me safe. 'I didn't know what I was doing. I was dreaming. I was sleepwalking.'

Thirty-two

Doctor Death faced me across the kitchen table. He touched my hand with his long curved fingers. I caught the scent of tobacco that surrounded him. I saw the black spots on his skin. Dad was telling him the story: my disappearance in the night, my sleepwalking. I heard in his voice how scared he still was, how he thought he'd lost me. I wanted to tell him again that I was all right, everything was all right.

'I woke up and knew he was gone. Straight away I knew he was gone. When you love somebody you know these things. It's right, Dan. Isn't it?'

Doctor Death tried to smile but his eyes stayed stupid and cold.

'And there was this girl with you?' he said.

'Mina,' said Dad. 'She saw him from her window, sleep-walking in the night. She went to help him. That's true, isn't it, Michael?'

I nodded.

Doctor Death licked his lips.

'Mina. She isn't one of mine,' he said. 'I wouldn't know her.'

He tried to smile again.

'Sleepwalking?' he said. He raised his eyebrows. 'And this is true?'

I stared at him.

'Yes. This is true.'

He watched me. He was cold, dry, pale as death. Wings would never rise at his back.

'Let me look at you.'

I stood in front of him. He shone a tiny bright torch into my eyes and peered into me. He shone it into my ears. I felt his breath and his scent all over me. He lifted my shirt and pressed his stethoscope against my chest and listened to me. I felt his clammy hands on my skin.

'What day is it?' he asked me. 'What month is it? What's the name of the Prime Minister?'

Dad chewed his lips as he watched and listened.

'Good lad,' he murmured as I answered.

Doctor Death touched my cheek.

'Is there anything you'd like to tell me?' he asked.

I shook my head.

'Don't be shy,' he said. 'Me and your Dad have been through everything you're going through.'

I shook my head again.

'He's a fit and healthy lad,' he said. 'Just keep an eye on him.' His mouth grinned as he looked at me. 'And make sure he stays in bed at night.'

He kept me close to him.

'It's a difficult time,' he said. 'Everything inside you's

changing. The world can seem a wild and weird place. But you'll get through it.'

'Did you treat Ernie?' I asked.

He raised his eyebrows.

'Ernie Myers. The man who lived here before.'

'Ah,' said Doctor Death. 'Yes, Mr Myers was one of mine.'

'Did he talk about seeing things?'

'Things?'

'Strange things. In the garden, in the house.'

From the corner of my eye I saw Dad chewing his lips again.

'Mr Myers was very ill,' said Doctor Death. 'He was dying.'

'I know that.'

'And as the mind approaches death it changes. It becomes less . . . orderly.'

'So he did?'

'He did speak of certain images that came to him. But so do many of my people.'

He held me again with his long fingers.

'I think you need to play football with your friends,' he said. 'I think you need to go to school again.' He looked at Dad. 'Yes, I think he should go to school again. Too much inside the house.' He tapped my head. 'Too much thinking and wondering and worrying going on in there.'

He stood up and Dad went with him to the door. I heard them muttering together in the hallway.

'School for you tomorrow,' said Dad as he came back in. He was trying to be all brisk and efficient but he pressed his lips together and looked at me and I saw the scared look in his eyes.

'I'm sorry, Dad,' I whispered.

We held each other tight, then we looked out at the wilderness.

'Why did you ask those things about Ernie?' he said.

'Don't know,' I said. 'Daft notions.'

'It's true, what you told us? That you were sleepwalking?'

For a moment I wanted to tell him everything: Skellig, the owls, what Mina and I got up to in the night. Then I knew how weird it would seem.

'Yes,' I said. 'It's true, Dad.'

Thirty-three

I did go to school next day. Rasputin started his lesson by welcoming me back. He said I'd missed a lot, but he hoped I'd be able to catch up. I told him I'd been studying evolution, and that I'd found out about the archaeopteryx. He raised his eyebrows.

'Do you think there are things like the archaeopteryx in the human world?' I asked him.

He peered at me.

'Humans that are turning into creatures that can fly?' I said.

I heard Coot sniggering behind me.

'Tell him about the monkey girl,' he said.

'What's that?' said Rasputin.

'The monkey girl,' said Coot.

I heard Leakey telling him to shut up.

'Maybe there's beings that's left over from the apes,' said Coot. 'Monkey girls and monkey boys.'

I ignored him.

'Our bones would need to become pneumatised,' I said.

Rasputin came to me and tousled my hair.

'Wings might help, as well,' he said. 'But I can see you've been reading widely. Well done, Michael. And stop interrupting, Coot. We all know who the monkey boy is here.'

Coot giggled. He grunted like an ape as Rasputin turned and went back to the front. He said we were past evolution now. We'd moved on to studying our own insides: the muscles, the heart and lungs, the digestive system, the nervous system, the brain.

'Keep coming to school, Michael,' he said. 'You don't want to miss anything more.'

'No, sir,' I said.

He unrolled a long poster of a cut-away man, bright-red lungs and heart exposed in his chest, stomach and intestines, networks of blood vessels and nerves, maroon muscles and white bones, blue-grey brain. He stared out at us through cavernous eyes. A few of the others shuddered in disgust.

'This is you,' said Rasputin.

Coot giggled.

Rasputin called him to the front. He acted out stripping Coot's skin away, tearing open his chest.

'Yes,' he said. 'Inside we're all the same, no matter how horrible the outside may seem to be. This is what we would see were we to open up our Mr Coot.'

He smiled.

'Of course, there may be a little more mess than appears in the picture.'

Coot scuttled back to his desk.

'Now,' said Rasputin. 'I'd like you to place your hand on

the left side on your chest like this. Feel the beating of your heart . . .'

We felt our hearts. I knew how stupid it would be to tell Rasputin that I could feel two hearts: the baby's and my own.

'This is our engine,' said Rasputin. 'Beating day and night, when we're awake and when we're sleeping. We don't have to think about it. Mostly we're hardly aware that it's even there. But if it stopped . . .'

Coot squawked, as if he'd been strangled.

'Correct, Mr Coot.'

Rasputin squawked too, and flopped across his desk.

I looked around. Half the class lay sprawled across their desks, pretending to be dead.

Leakey was watching me. I could tell he wanted to be friends again.

In the yard that lunchtime, I played football as hard as I could. I did sliding tackles and diving headers. I dribbled and dummied and went for wild overhead kicks. I scored four goals, made three more and my team won by miles. At the end there was a long rip down the side of my jeans. The knuckles of my left hand were scratched and scraped. There was blood trickling from a little cut over my eye.

The lads on my team surrounded me as we headed back inside. They said it was the best I'd ever played. They told me I should stop staying off. They needed me.

'Don't worry,' said Leakey. 'He's really back this time, aren't you, Michael?'

We had Miss Clarts in the afternoon. I wrote a story about

a boy exploring some abandoned warehouses by the river. He finds an old stinking tramp who turns out to have wings growing under his ancient coat. The boy feeds the man with sandwiches and chocolate and the man becomes strong again. The boy has a friend called Kara. The man teaches the boy and Kara how it feels to fly, and then he disappears, flapping away across the water.

I saw the tears in Miss Clarts' eyes as she sat beside me and read the story.

'It's lovely, Michael,' she said. 'Your style is really coming on. You've been practising at home?'

I nodded.

'Good,' she said. 'You have a true gift. Look after it.'

It was just after this that the secretary, Mrs Moore, came in and whispered something to Miss Clarts. They both looked at me. Mrs Moore asked me to go with her for a moment. I was trembling as I went to her. I put my hand on my chest and felt my heart. She led me through the long corridors towards her office. My dad was on the phone, she said. He wanted a word with me.

I chewed my lips as I lifted the handset.

I heard him breathing, sighing.

'It's the baby,' I said.

'Yes. Something's not right. I need to go in, to sort things out.'

'Something?'

'A lot of things, son. They want to talk to me and your mum together.'

'Not me?'

'I talked to Mina's mum. You can have tea there. You can wait there till I come home. I'll not be long. You'll hardly know I've been away.'

'Will the baby be all right?'

'They think so. They hope so. Anyway, nothing will happen tonight. It's tomorrow they'll be doing it.'

'I should have stayed at home. I should have kept thinking about her.'

'I'll give her a kiss from you.'

'And Mum.'

'And Mum. You're very brave, Michael.'

No, I'm not, I thought as I felt myself trembling. No, I'm blinking not.

Thirty-four

I sat at the kitchen table with Mina. Her mother was above us, cutting up lettuce and tomatoes and bread. The table was spread with paper and paints. Mina had been painting all afternoon. There were little streaks of paint on her face. Her fingers were bright with daubs of colour. There was a large drawing of Skellig, standing erect with his wings high above his shoulders. He gazed out at us, smiling.

'What if she sees?' I whispered.

'It could be anyone,' said Mina. 'Or anything.'

Her mother turned towards us.

'Good, isn't it, Michael?' she said.

I nodded.

'The kind of thing William Blake saw. He said we were surrounded by angels and spirits. We must just open our eyes a little wider, look a little harder.'

She pulled a book from a shelf, showed me Blake's pictures of the winged beings he saw in his little home in London.

'Maybe we could all see such beings, if only we knew how to,' she said.

She touched my cheek.

'But it's enough for me to have you two angels at my table.'

She stared hard at us, making her eyes wide and unblinking.

'Yes,' she smiled. 'Isn't it amazing? I see you clearly, two angels at my table.'

I thought of the baby. I wondered what she would see, with her innocent eyes. I wondered what she would see, if she were near to death.

I turned my mind away from her. I pulled a sheet of paper towards me. I found myself drawing Coot, giving him twisted arms and legs and bright red hair. I drew hair sprouting from his back, his chest, his legs.

'That's your friend,' said Mina. 'A proper little demon.'

I looked at her, looked just past her, wanting to see her ghostly wings again. Her mother started singing:

> 'I dreamt a dream! What can it mean?
> And that I was a maiden Queen . . .'

'I went back to him today,' Mina whispered.

I drew horns growing from Coot's skull.

'I came for you first,' she said. 'Your dad said you'd gone to school. Shouldn't I be working? he asked. Shouldn't I be at my lessons?'

She leaned over and drew a skinny black tongue protruding from Coot's mouth.

'Guarded by an Angel mild
Witless woe, was ne'er beguil'd!'

'Skellig said, "Where's Michael?" ' whispered Mina. ' "At school," I said. "School!" he said. "He abandons me for school!" I said you hadn't abandoned him. I said you loved him.'

'I do,' I whispered.

'I said how terrified you were that the baby might die.'

'She won't,' I said. 'She mustn't.'

'He says you must keep coming to see him.'

She chewed her lip, leaned closer.

'He says he's going away soon, Michael.'

'So he took his wings and fled:
Then the morn blush'd rosy red.'

'Going away?' I said.

'Yes.'

'Where to?'

She shook her head.

'He wouldn't say.'

'When?'

'Soon.'

My hands were trembling. I grabbed some more paper. I drew Skellig, flapping across a pale sky.

'Soon my Angel came again;
I was arm'd, he came in vain . . .'

Her mother leaned over us, began clearing a space to put down our plates.

' "For the time of youth was fled," ' she sang, ' "And grey hairs were on my head." '

'Come on,' she said. 'Bunk up. Food's ready. That's a lovely picture, Michael.'

Thirty-five

We waited at the table as the light faded, and Dad didn't come. I kept going to the front room, looking out into the street, seeing nothing. Mina's mother kept comforting me.

'Don't worry, Michael. He'll come soon. Don't worry, Michael. I'm sure everything's all right.'

We drew and drew. I drew my family gathered around the baby. I drew Mina with her pale face, her dark eyes, the black fringe of her hair cut dead straight across her brow. I drew Skellig lying dry and dusty and useless on the garage floor, then I drew him standing proudly by the arched window with the owls flying around him. I stared at the changed Skellig. How had this happened to him? Was it just Chinese food and cod liver oil and aspirin and brown ale and dead things left by owls? I drew Ernie Myers in striped pyjamas looking out into the wilderness. I felt how the more I drew, the more my hand and arm became free. I saw how what appeared on the page looked more and more like what I saw or what I thought of in my head. I felt how by drawing my mind became concentrated, even while one part of it still thought about and worried about the baby. I drew the baby time and again, sometimes focusing on her wide, bold eyes, sometimes on her tiny hands, sometimes on the way her whole body arched when she rested on your knee. I drew the world as the baby might see it: the long hospital ward filled with lumbering adults, the networks of wires and tubes and bleeping instruments filling the foreground, the faces of nurses smiling down. I drew the world twisted into weird shapes by the curved glass case that covered her. In the end, I drew Skellig at the door to the ward. I felt the burst of excitement she would feel to see this, the quickening of her heart, the flickering of her life.

Mina looked at my drawings, one after the other. She made a pile of them before her. She gripped my hand.

'You couldn't have done these before,' she said. 'You're getting braver and bolder.'

I shrugged.

'You get better at playing football by playing football,' I said. 'You get better at drawing by drawing.'

We waited and waited. The light fell. The blackbirds sang in the trees and hedges outside. Mina's mother switched a lamp on. The phone rang but it wasn't Dad. Mina's mother gave us little squares of chocolate that I allowed to melt slowly and gently on my tongue. She kept singing songs from time to time. Some of them were songs of Blake's, some were ancient folk songs. Mina joined in sometimes, with her bold high voice.

'The sun descending in the west.
The evening star does shine.
The birds are silent in their nest,
And I must seek for mine . . .'

Mina smiled at my silence.

'Soon we'll have you singing, too,' she said.

The day darkened and darkened.

'I want to show you something,' said Mina.

She filled a little bowl with warm water and put it on the table. She reached up on to the shelf and took down a ball of skin and bone and fur, like the one she had taken from the garage floor. She dropped it into the warm water. She rubbed it with her fingers. It separated into fragments of dark fur and ripped skin. She pulled out tiny bones. There was a skull, the skull of a tiny animal.

Her mother watched and smiled.

'Another owl pellet,' she said.

'Yes,' said Mina. She looked at me. 'Owls eat their victims whole, Michael,' she said. 'They digest the flesh. Then they regurgitate the parts that can't be digested. Skin and bone and fur. You can see what the owl has been eating by inspecting the pellet. This owl, like most owls, has eaten small creatures, like mice or voles.'

Her mother turned away, worked at the sink.

'This is the pellet I brought out from the garage,' she whispered. 'There were dozens of them in there, Michael.'

'It came from Skellig,' I whispered.

She nodded.

'What does it mean?'

She shook her head.

'What is he?'

She shook her head.

There was nothing more I could say.

'Extraordinary!' she hissed.

She started singing again.

When I looked out into the street I saw lights in windows, the tree-tops etched black against the mauve sky. I looked up and saw the last birds heading for their nests.

Then the phone went again and this time it was Dad. Mina's mother held the handset out to me. I couldn't go to it.

She smiled.

'Come on,' she said. 'Come on.'

Dad said everything was fine. The baby was sleeping. He'd seen the doctors. He was staying for a little while longer with Mum.

'Is the baby OK?' I said. 'What are they going to do?'

'They'll operate tomorrow,' he said.

'What are they going to do?'

No answer.

'Dad. What are they going to do?'

I heard the sighing, the fear in his voice.

'They're operating on her heart, Michael.'

He said some more but I couldn't hear it. Something about being with me soon, about how everything would be fine, about how Mum sent me her love. I dropped the phone.

'They're operating on her heart,' I whispered.

Thirty-six

I went out into the front garden with Mina. We sat on the front wall waiting for Dad's car turning into the street. The door was open behind us, letting a wedge of light out into the dark. Whisper came, slinking through the shadows below the wall. He sat below us, curled against our feet.

'What does it mean,' I said, 'If Skellig eats living things and makes pellets like the owls?'

She shrugged.

'We can't know,' she said.

'What is he?' I said.

'We can't know. Sometimes we just have to accept there are things we can't know. Why is your sister ill? Why did my father die?' She held my hand. 'Sometimes we think we should be able to know everything. But we can't. We have to allow ourselves to see what there is to see, and we have to imagine.'

We talked about the fledglings in the nest above us. We tried together to hear their breathing. We wondered what blackbird babies dreamed about.

'Sometimes they'll be very scared,' said Mina. 'They'll dream about cats climbing towards them. They'll dream about dangerous crows with ugly beaks. They'll dream about vicious children plundering the nest. They'll dream of death all around them. But there'll be happy dreams as well. Dreams of life. They'll dream of flying like their parents do. They'll dream of finding their own tree one day, building their own nest, having their own chicks.'

I held my hand to my heart. What would I feel when they opened the baby's fragile chest, when they cut into her tiny heart? Mina's fingers were cold and dry and small. I felt the tiny pulse of blood in them. I felt how my own hand trembled very quickly, very gently.

'We're still like chicks,' she said. 'Happy half the time, half the time dead scared.'

I closed my eyes and tried to discover where the happy half was hiding. I felt the tears trickling through my tightly closed eyelids. I felt Whisper's claws tugging at my jeans. I wanted to be all alone in an attic like Skellig, with just the owls and the moonlight and an oblivious heart.

'You're so brave,' said Mina.

And then Dad's car came, with its blaring engine and its glaring lights, and the fear just increased and increased and increased.

Thirty-seven

An endless night. In and out of dreams. In and out of sleep. Dad snoring and snuffling in the room next door. No moon in the sky. Endless darkness. The clock at my bedside was surely stuck. All it showed were the dead hours. One o'clock. Two o'clock. Three o'clock. Endless minutes between them. No hooting of owls, no calling from Skellig or Mina. Like the whole world was stuck, all of time was stuck. Then I must have slept properly at last, and I woke to daylight with stinging eyes and sunken heart.

And then we fought, my Dad and I, while we crunched burnt toast and swigged tepid tea.

'No!' I yelled. 'I won't go to school! Why should I? Not today!'

'You'll do as you're bloody told! You'll do what's best for your mum and the baby!'

'You just want me out of the way so you don't have to think about me and don't have to worry about me and you can just think about the bloody baby!'

'Don't say bloody!'

'It is bloody! It's bloody bloody bloody! And it isn't fair!'

Dad kicked the leg of the table and the milk bottle toppled over on the table and a jar of jam crashed to the floor.

'See?' he yelled. 'See the state you get me in?'

He raised his fists like he wanted to smash something: anything, the table, me.

'Go to bloody school!' he yelled. 'Get out my bloody sight!'

Then he just reached across and grabbed me to him.

'I love you,' he whispered. 'I love you.'

And we cried and cried.

'You could come with me,' he said. 'But there'd be nothing you could do. We just have to wait and pray and believe that everything will be all right.'

Moments later, Mina came knocking at the door.

She had Whisper in her arms.

'You've got to come and help me,' she said.

Dad nodded.

'I'll come for you this afternoon,' he said. 'When the operation's over. Go with Mina.'

She took me to her garden. She gripped Whisper tight. On the rooftop, the blackbird started yelling its alarm call.

'Bad boy,' she said to the cat, and she went to the open front door, threw him in, pushed it shut behind him.

'The fledglings are out,' she said. 'Stay dead still and quiet. Watch out for cats.'

We sat on the front step and didn't move.

'Under the hedge,' she said. 'And under the rose tree by the wall.'

I started to ask what I was looking for, but then I saw the first of them, little brown feathered ball with its beak gaping in the darkness beneath the hedge.

'This is how they start their life outside the nest,' she said. 'They can't fly. Their parents still have to feed them. But they're nearly all alone. All they can do is walk and hide in the shadows and wait for their food.'

The parents came closer, the brown mother to the lowest branch of the tree, the jet black father to the top of the hedge. Worms dangled from their beaks. They called softly to each other and the fledglings with little clicks and coughs.

'First day out,' whispered Mina. 'Think Whisper's had at least one of them already.'

The parents waited, wary of us, then at last they dropped into the garden. A fledgling tottered out from beneath the rose bush, let its mother drop the worms into its beak, tottered back again. The father fed the one beneath the hedge. The parents flew away again.

'They'll be doing this all day,' said Mina. 'Flying and feeding all the way till dusk. And the same thing tomorrow and tomorrow till the chicks can fly.'

We stayed watching.

'Cats'll get them,' she said. 'Or crows, or stupid dogs.'

Dad came out of our house. He came into Mina's garden. Mina pressed a finger to her lips and widened her eyes in warning. He tiptoed to us.

‘The fledglings are out of the nest,’ she whispered.

She showed him where to look.

‘Yes,’ he whispered. ‘Yes. Yes.’

He crouched beside us, dead still.

‘Aren’t they lovely?’ he said.

He cupped my cheek in his hand and we looked deep into each other’s eyes. Then he had to go.

‘You just keep believing,’ he said. ‘And everything will be fine.’

He went to the car and drove from the street as quietly as he could. Mina and I watched and waited as the brown mother and the jet-black father flew in and out of the garden, feeding their young.

Thirty-eight

Mid morning. Mina's mother brought cups of tea for us. She sat beside us on the step. She talked about the fledglings, the flowers that were bursting into bloom, the air that every day became warmer, the sun that every day was a little higher and a little warmer. She talked about the way spring made the world burst into life after months of apparent death. She told us about the goddess called Persephone, who was forced to spend half a year in the darkness deep underground. Winter happened when she was trapped inside the earth. The days shrank, they became cold and short and dark. Living things hid themselves away. Spring came when she was released and made her slow way up to the world again. The world became brighter and bolder in order to welcome her back. It began to be filled with warmth and light. The animals dared to wake, they dared to have their young. Plants dared to send out buds and shoots. Life dared to come back.

'An old myth,' I said.

'Yes,' she said. 'But maybe it's a myth that's nearly true. Look around you, Michael. Fledglings and blooms and bright sunshine. Maybe what we see around us is the whole world welcoming Persephone home.'

She rested her hand on my arm.

'They can do marvellous things, Michael. Maybe you'll soon be welcoming your own Persephone home.'

We thought of Persephone for a while in silence. I imagined her struggling her way towards us. She squeezed through black tunnels. She took wrong turnings, banged her head against the rocks. Sometimes she gave up in despair and she just lay weeping in the pitch darkness. But she struggled on. She waded through icy underground streams. She fought through bedrock and clay and iron ore and coal, through fossils of ancient creatures, the skeletons of dinosaurs, the buried remains of ancient cities. She burrowed past the tangled roots of great trees. She was torn and bleeding but she kept telling herself to move onward and upward. She told herself that soon she'd see the light of the sun again and feel the warmth of the world again.

Then Mina's mother broke into my thoughts.

'I'll watch the birds,' she said. 'Why don't you both go and wander for a while?'

And Mina took my hand, and led me away.

It was like walking in a dream. The houses tilted and swayed. The sun glared over the rooftops. Birds were ragged and black against the astonishing sky. The roadway glistened, a deep black pond. Invisible traffic roared and squealed.

She held my arm.

'Are you all right, Michael?' she kept asking. 'Are you sure you're all right?'

We made our way towards the DANGER door. She led me through the gate, through the long garden, through the door, into the dark and dusty interior. We went up in silence. She held my arm, like I was an old man, or an invalid.

On the final landing she told me,

'He'll be waiting for us, Michael. He'll be so pleased to see you again.'

She turned the handle, we went in, sunlight poured through the arched window.

We stood there staring.

He wasn't there.

Mina ran back down through the house. I heard her feet on the bare boards, doors swinging open. I heard her calling for him.

'Skellig! Skellig! Skellig!'

I heard her coming slowly back up to me. Her face was paler than ever. There were tears shining in her eyes.

'He isn't here,' she whispered. 'He just isn't here at all.'

We went to the window and gazed into the empty sky above the city.

I found myself falling forward. I gripped the windowsill tight. I touched my heart.

'Oh, Mina!' I said.

'What is it?'

'My heart's stopped. Feel my heart. There's nothing there.'

She caught her breath. She touched my chest. She called my name.

And then there was just blackness.

Thirty-nine

'Don't call Doctor Death,' I murmured. 'Don't call Doctor Death.'

I was slumped on the floorboards. Mina was kneeling over me. She stroked my brow, whispered my name.

'Not Doctor Death,' I said again.

'No,' she said. 'Not Doctor Death.'

I struggled to sit up. I leaned against the wall beneath the window.

'Touch your heart,' she said.

I did this, and I felt the beating there.

'See?' she said.

'But it's only mine. It's not the baby's.'

'Oh, Michael.'

I felt my strength coming back to me. I swallowed, squeezed my eyes, tightened my fists. I felt my heart again.

'It's only my heart, Mina. Not the baby's. The baby's dead.'

'You can't know for certain,' she said.

I pulled myself to my feet.

'I think I can, Mina.'

She held me as we went out of the room and into the darkness of the house.

'Where is he?' I asked as we went down.

No answer.

'You looked everywhere?' I said.

'Yes, everywhere.'

I touched my heart again and it was still the same.

'She's dead,' I whispered.

'But maybe she's fine.'

'I'll phone the hospital,' I said, but I knew I wouldn't dare.

We went out into the spring light. As we stepped out, we saw blackbird fledglings tottering into the cover of hedges. In the lane, an unknown cat hunched behind a dustbin, and watched us pass with hostile eyes.

'Your dad'll come for you soon,' said Mina. 'He'll tell you everything's fine.'

'Don't tell him about me,' I said. 'He doesn't need to worry about me.'

She smiled and squeezed me tight.

'Where the hell's Skellig?' I said.

She shook her head and we walked on. Miles above us, a great heavy bird flapped across the blue.

'William Blake used to faint sometimes,' said Mina. 'He said the soul was able to leap out of the body for a while, and then leap back again. He said it could be caused by great fear or enormous pain. Sometimes it was because of too much joy. It was possible to be overwhelmed by the presence of so much beauty in the world.'

We walked on. My body was heavy and awkward, like I was arthritic, like I was turning to stone.

'I think you understand that,' she said.

I couldn't speak. My mouth was dry and sour, like I'd swallowed the owls' leavings from the windowsill.

'Yes,' she said. 'That's what he said. The soul leaps out and then leaps back again.' She laughed. 'It's like a dance.'

We went back to Mina's house. We sat on the step and watched the fledglings.

'Maybe he's gone away for ever, like he said he would,' I said.

I held my hand against my heart, and we waited for Dad to come home.

Forty

Mina's mother rested a wooden board on her knees. She smiled and put a pomegranate on the board.

'Pomegranate,' she said. 'Isn't it a lovely word?'

She cut through the fruit with a kitchen knife. The red juice leaked out. The hundreds of seeds inside were exposed.

'It's what Persephone ate while she was waiting in the Underworld,' she said.

She gave a quarter to me, a quarter to Mina, and took a quarter for herself. She gave us pins to pick the pips out with, and we sat there nibbling away the sweet flesh from the bitter seed.

'Look at all the life in this,' she said. 'Every pip could become a tree, and every tree could bear another hundred fruits and every fruit could bear another hundred trees. And so on to infinity.'

I picked the pips from my tongue with my fingers.

'Just imagine,' she said. 'If every seed grew, there'd be no room in the world for anything but pomegranate trees.'

I licked my lips. Mina sat close against me. We watched

the blackbirds returning time and again to feed their young. I watched the sky and imagined Skellig flying away, a tiny black speck travelling over the endless curves of the world. The phone rang and my heart thudded and raced as Mina's mother went inside, but it wasn't Dad.

I picked seed after seed from the fruit.

'How's your heart?' whispered Mina.

I tried to find the baby's gentle beat beneath my fast and frightened thud.

I shook my head.

'She isn't there.'

The sun climbed through the sky, became warmer, warmer.

Soon Mrs Dando cycled into the street and saw us sitting there. She bustled into the garden while the blackbirds squawked their warning calls from the rooftop and the fledglings scuttled into cover.

'Such a lovely day,' she said.

She beamed at us.

'We're all missing you again,' she said.

Mina's mother gave her the final quarter of the pomegranate and she nibbled the seeds and giggled.

'Pomegranates,' she said. 'Not had one of these since I was a girl of twelve.'

She told me about Leakey and Coot and all the others.

'They keep telling me – "Get Michael to come back." '

She gave me a new folder of work. There was a drawing of the opened body with arrows pointing to its parts. Rasputin's note told me to write the missing names.

Mina and I looked at the drawing together.

'Tibia,' we said. 'Fibula, sternum, clavicle, radius, ulna, kidneys, liver, lungs, heart, brain.'

'And spirit jumping in and jumping out but never seen,' said Mina.

Mrs Dando looked at her. I knew that Coot would have talked to Mrs Dando about her. A daft monkey girl, he'd have said. The lass that sits in a tree like a crow. The lass that's keeping him away.

Miss Clarts had written, 'Write another story like the last one, Michael. Something just as lovely. Let your imagination fly.'

I closed my eyes. I wanted to imagine nothing. The baby was dead. Skellig was gone. The world that was left was ugly, cold, terrifying. The blackbirds squawked and squawked while Mrs Dando told Mina's mother about what a great footballer I was, about how I loved having a daft time with the other boys.

Mina's mother smiled.

'How's the baby?' Mrs Dando said at last.

'Don't know,' I whispered.

'She's having an operation today,' said Mina.

'Oh, poor little soul,' said Mrs Dando.

'Yes,' said Mina. 'And to be quite honest, Mrs Dando, the last thing Michael needs is to be troubled by petty things like football and school.'

Her mother sighed.

'Mina,' she said.

'Well,' said Mina. 'Isn't it true? Michael?'

I couldn't stand it. I went to sit on the front wall, facing away from them.

'See?' said Mina. 'See how you've upset him?'

And then Dad drove into the street and parked the car in front of me. He held the door open. I got in beside him. He put his arm around me.

'It's over, son,' he said.

Forty-one

I was wrong. She wasn't dead. She was in a long, deep sleep that followed the anaesthetic. She was snoring gently beneath white blankets. Mum told us about the great wound in her tiny chest and the massive bandage that covered it. There were wires and tubes again and a machine that bleeped in rhythm with her tiny heart.

'They said everything'll be all right now, Michael,' she said. 'They're sure everything'll be all right.'

We sat there, the three of us, hand in hand, looking down at the delicate creature.

'They said there was a moment when they thought they'd lost her,' she said. She put her arm around me. 'But she burst into life again.'

A nurse came. She checked the wires and tubes and the machine. She patted my head.

'Your sister's got a heart of fire,' she said. 'She's a little fighter. She won't give in.'

'You still say your prayers for her?' asked Mum.

'Yes,' I said.

‘We’ve been wondering again what to call her,’ said Dad.

‘Persephone,’ I said.

They laughed.

‘Too much of a mouthful,’ he said.

‘It has to be something very little and very strong,’ Mum said. ‘Just like she is.’

‘Gus,’ said Dad, and we giggled.

‘Butch,’ I said.

‘Garth,’ said Mum.

‘Buster,’ said Dad.

‘Look,’ said Mum. ‘She’s dreaming.’

And she was. Her eyes were moving behind their lids.

‘Wonder what she sees,’ said Dad.

‘Only nice things, I hope,’ said Mum.

‘I’m sure that’s right,’ said Dad. ‘Look at her face. Sweet and still, nearly smiling. Little angel. I know. We could call her Angela. But no, too long.’

‘It was the strangest thing,’ said Mum.

She stopped and shook her head.

‘What was?’ said Dad.

She crinkled her face up, like she was embarrassed.

‘Well,’ she said. ‘I was lying here last night, tossing and turning. Kept getting up to look at her. Kept dropping off to sleep. And the strangest of dreams . . .’

‘And . . .?’ said Dad.

‘And I saw this man, that’s all. Another dream, though I was sure I was wide awake. He was standing over the baby. He was filthy. All in black, an ancient dusty suit. A great hunch on his back. Hair all matted and tangled. I was terrified. I wanted to reach out to him. I wanted to push him away. I wanted to scream, Get away from our baby! I wanted to shout for the nurses and the doctors. But I couldn't move, couldn't speak, and I was sure he was going to take her away. But then he turned and looked at me. His face as white and dry as chalk. And there was such tenderness in his eyes. And for some reason I knew he hadn't come to harm her. I knew it would be all right . . .'

She stopped again and shook her head.

'And . . .?' said Dad.

'And then he reached right down with both hands and lifted her up. She was wide awake. They stared and stared into each other's eyes. He started slowly to turn around . . .'

'Like they were dancing,' I said.

'That's right, like they were dancing. And then the strangest thing of all . . .'

She laughed at us, and shrugged.

'And the strangest thing of all was, there were wings on the baby's back. Not solid wings. Transparent, ghostly, hardly visible, but there they were. Little feathery things. It looked so funny. The strange tall man and the little baby and the wings. And that was it. He put her back down, he turned and looked at me again, and it was over. I slept like a log the rest of the night. When I woke up they were already getting her ready for the operation. But I wasn't worried any more. I kissed her and whispered to her how much we all loved her and they took her away. I knew it was going to be all right.'

'And it is,' said Dad.

'And it is.'

She poked me in the ribs.

'Must have been thinking about what you asked me. What are shoulder blades for? Eh?'

I smiled and nodded.

'Yes. Yes.'

The baby's eyes kept moving, seeing the things she imagined in her sleep.

'Funny little chick,' said Dad. 'What can she be seeing?'

'Skellig,' I whispered to myself. 'Skellig.'

'It isn't over,' said Mum. 'You know that, don't you? We'll have to protect her always, especially at first.'

'I know,' I said. 'We'll love her and love her and love her.'

We left soon afterwards. In the corridor I saw Doctor MacNabola coming out of the lift with a clutch of students in white coats around him. I told Dad just to wait a minute. I ran to Doctor MacNabola. He looked down at me.

'Doctor,' I said. 'I told you about my friend. Remember? The one with arthritis.'

He puffed his chest out and drew his shoulders up.

'Aha,' he said. 'So is he ready for my needles and my saw?'

'No,' I said. 'He seems to be getting better.'

'Splendid,' he said. 'Cod liver oil and a dose of positive thinking, eh? Maybe he'll escape me yet.'

The students giggled.

'Can love help a person to get better?' I asked.

He raised his eyebrows, pursed his lips, tapped his chin.

One of the students took a notebook and pencil from her pocket.

'Love,' said the doctor. 'Hmmm. What can we doctors know about love, eh?' He winked at the student with the notebook and she blushed. ' "Love is the child that breathes our breath/Love is the child that scatters death." '

'William Blake?' I said.

He laughed.

'We have an educated man before us,' he said.

He smiled properly for the first time.

'Tell your friend that I hope he and I never have to meet.'

Then he winked at me, turned, and led the students away.

'What was that about?' said Dad when I hurried back to him.

'Nothing,' I said. 'Somebody I met soon after the baby came in.'

He laughed.

'Mystery man, that's who you are.'

In the car on the way home we wound the windows down and he sang 'The Black Hills of Dakota' at the top of his voice. I put my hands together and hooted and hooted like an owl.

'That's good,' he said. 'I like that. That's really good. You'll have to show me how to do that one. Not while I'm driving, though, eh?'

We smiled as we drove through the busy city streets.

'She's not out of danger yet,' he said. 'You do understand that, don't you?'

'Yes. But she will be, won't she?'

'Yes!' he yelled. 'Yes, she blinking will!'

And he sang again.

'Have to get on with that blinking house now, eh?' he said. 'I know! We can have 27 and 53 tonight, eh?'

'27 and 53,' I said. 'Sweetest of nectars!'

'Sweetest of nectars! I like that. Sweetest of blinking nectars!'

Forty-two

It was long after dusk when Mina and I went out with the remnants of 27 and 53 and a bottle of brown ale in a paper bag. The lights were on in the streets, the air was cold, and the sky was glittering with stars. Our breath curled in long white plumes around us. I told Mina about Mum's dream as we walked.

'Extraordinary,' she whispered.

She smiled and said it showed that he'd always be there, whenever we might need him. But we knew we wanted to see him and touch him again.

In the lane, we found Whisper at our heels.

'Bad boy,' she said, leaning down to stroke him.

She laughed.

'All day long the fledglings got stronger and braver. They fluttered up into the middle of the hedge where they couldn't be caught. All day long they were getting worms, worms, worms, and when we let him out, this one just sat grumpy and frustrated on the step beside us.'

She stroked him again.

'Horrible little savage,' she said, and he purred and pressed against her.

We went through the DANGER door expecting nothing. The house was still and silent. The attic was empty. No owls. No Skellig. On the windowsill we found a dead mouse, a bit of bacon rind, a little mound of dead black beetles.

We sat on the floor against the wall and stared out towards the endless stars.

'I really think she'll be all right now,' I said.

Mina smiled and Whisper purred.

'Feel my heart,' I said.

She put her hand on my chest.

'Can you feel it?' I said. 'Her heart beating right in there beside my own?'

She concentrated.

'I'm not sure, Michael,' she said.

'Try again. Concentrate. It's like touching and listening and imagining all at the same time. It's something far-off and tiny, like blackbird chicks cheeping in a nest.'

She closed her eyes and felt again.

She smiled.

'Yes,' she whispered. 'Yes, there it is. There and there and there.'

'The baby's heart,' I said. 'It won't stop now.'

'It won't stop now.'

She started singing her William Blake song.

'The sun descending in the west.

The evening star does shine . . .'

I joined in with her.

'The birds are silent in their nest
And I must seek for mine . . .'

'See?' she said. 'I said we'd get you singing.'

The night deepened and we knew we'd have to go home soon.

'I could sleep here,' she said. 'Just like this. And be happy for ever.'

I sighed.

'But we have to go.'

We didn't move.

And then there was a sudden rustling in the air outside, the stars were blocked out, the window creaked, and there he was, climbing in through the arched frame. He didn't see us. He crouched on the floor, gasping for breath. His wings slowly settled on his back.

'Skellig,' I hissed.

He turned his moon-pale face towards us.

'Michael. Mina,' he said. His voice was shallow, thin, strained, but a smile was forming on his face.

I held out the paper bag.

'We brought you this, Skellig. 27 and 53.'

'Ha!'

I opened the bag and we took it to him. We knelt at his side. He hooked his long curved finger into the food, lifted out a string of sauce and pork and beansprouts. He licked it from his finger with his long pale tongue.

'Sweetest of nectars,' he whispered. 'Food of the blinking gods.'

'And this,' I said.

I snapped the top off the bottle and he let me trickle the beer into his open mouth.

'Thought it was cold mice for supper and I come home to a banquet.'

He ate again, sighed with contentment.

'Pair of angels,' he said. 'That's what you are.'

We watched him eat and drink, saw him gathering his strength.

'You went to my sister,' I said.

He laughed.

'Hm! Pretty little thing.'

'You made her strong.'

'That one's glittering with life. Heart like fire. It was her that gave the strength to me.'

He sipped at the beer again.

'But worn out now,' he said. 'Knackered.'

Then he reached out and touched Mina's face, then mine.

'But I'm getting strong, thanks to the angels and the owls.'

He put the food and drink aside and leaned against the wall.

We sat in a tiny circle, the three of us, and for minutes we just watched each other and smiled.

'You're going away,' I said at last.

He closed his eyes and nodded.

'Where will you go?' I said.

He shrugged, pointed out to the sky.

'Somewhere,' he said.

I touched his dry, cold hand.

'What are you?' I whispered.

He shrugged again.

'Something,' he said. 'Something like you, something like a beast, something like a bird, something like an angel.' He laughed. 'Something like that.'

He smiled.

'Let's stand up,' he said.

We made our circle and we held each other tight. We looked deep into each other's eyes. We began to turn. Our hearts and breath were together. We turned and turned until the ghostly wings rose from Mina's back and mine, until we felt ourselves being raised, until we seemed to turn and dance in the empty air.

And then it ended and we came to earth again.

'We'll remember for ever,' said Mina.

Skellig leaned forward and hugged us both.

He licked a drop of red sauce from his lips.

'Thank you for 27 and 53,' he said. 'Thank you for giving me my life again. Now you have to go home.'

We watched him as we walked towards the door and as we pulled it open. We peered through as we slowly pulled it closed. He gazed back at us with his tender eyes. Then we went silently down through the house and we stepped out with Whisper into the astounding night.

Forty-three

I was brilliant at school next day. Nobody could get the ball away from me. I did body swerves and dribbles and flicks. I skipped over tackles, back-heeled the ball to my team mates, scored with diving headers and with long shots curled into the corners of the net.

After the bell went, and we were trailing back to the school across the field, Leakey ran after me.

'Lucky sod,' he said. 'You'll never play like that again.'

I laughed.

'Luck? What about this, then?'

I dropped the ball and dribbled it round him. I flicked it between his legs and ran on with it. Then he got me with a thumping tackle into the back of my legs that sent us both sprawling.

'Foul!' I shouted. 'Foul!'

We started wrestling, rolling over and over on the grass. He was bigger than me and he pinned me down, sat over me, pressed my shoulders into the ground.

He was grinning.

'Say it again,' he said.

'Foul! Bloody foul!'

He lifted his fist like he was going to smash me in the face but then he just laughed and flopped down and lay beside me.

'Bloody hell,' he said. 'You were brilliant.'

We lay there laughing, then Mrs Dando started yelling.

'Get in, you two! You're going to be late!'

We walked together towards school.

'It's like you've been miles and miles away,' he said.

'I know,' I said.

'Would you tell me about it?' he said.

We paused and I looked at him and I knew he really wanted to know.

'Some day I'll tell you everything,' I said.

We saw Coot in the school doorway waiting for us.

'Might even tell that daft sod,' I said. 'If I think he might believe it.'

Then Mrs Dando was yelling again.

'Come on, you two! Come on! Get in!'

Forty-four

That evening and the evenings that followed, I helped Dad in the house. I mixed wallpaper paste for him and carefully painted door frames and window frames with him. We went to see Mum and the baby in the hospital. The baby soon came out of her long sleep and she got stronger and stronger. They took the wires and tubes out of her and they switched off the machine. The bandages on her chest were smaller and smaller. Every evening she sat in my lap, twisting and turning and gurgling. She learned how to stick out her tongue at us, and her mouth and eyes started to smile.

'Look at her,' we'd say. 'Little devil.'

And Mum would laugh and say, 'Watch out. We're coming home soon.'

I used to look for Dr MacNabola, but I never saw him again.

We had lots of Chinese takeaways. Dad winked and said we had to keep it quiet or Mum would have us on salad for a month. I poked his stomach.

'Mightn't be a bad idea, Fatso.'

'You don't want them, then?' he said. 'No more 27 and 53, then?'

'That's right, Fatso,' I said. 'I'll have . . . 19 and 42 instead.'

'Ha! A bit of imagination, eh?'

After we'd eaten, I'd go to Mina's. We drew and painted on her kitchen table. We read William Blake and we wrote stories about adventures in old houses and journeys to far-off imaginary places.

Each evening, Mina used to ask, 'When's she coming home, Michael? I can hardly wait. I haven't even seen her yet.'

We went one more time to the attic before the baby came home. The sun was still shining. It hung low and red and huge over the city.

The attic was empty and silent. She pointed to the heap of owl pellets beneath the nest.

'Don't go near,' she said. 'They'll defend their chicks to the death.'

We stood at the centre, remembering Skellig.

'Someone else might find him now,' said Mina.

'Yes,' I said. 'I hope they do.'

Then we saw the outline of a heart scratched into the floorboards beneath the arched window. Just outside the heart was scratched, *Thank you. S.*, and inside were three small white feathers.

We picked up the feathers and smiled.

'Three,' said Mina.

'One for the baby as well,' I said.

As we crouched there, the owls flew out into the room and perched on the frame above us. Then two fledglings appeared, tottering in the shadows by the far wall. They were round and almost naked. Little cheeps came from their wide open beaks. We gasped at how beautiful they were, how delicate. Then the owls went out hunting. We stayed for a while. We watched the owls flying back in with the meat from tiny animals they'd killed. We watched the fledglings gorge themselves.

'Little savages,' I said.

'That's right,' said Mina. 'Beautiful tender savages.'

We smiled, and prepared to tiptoe away. Then the owls flew back in and came to us. They laid something on the floor in front of us. A dead mouse, a tiny dead baby bird. Blood was still trickling through the ripped fur, through the young feathers. The owls flew quickly away again, and we heard them hooting in the thickening night.

'Savages,' I whispered.

'Killers,' said Mina. 'Extraordinary presents, eh.'

'They think we're something like them,' I said.

'Perhaps we are,' said Mina.

We lifted the creatures and tiptoed out.

'Goodnight, little chicks,' we whispered.

Outside, we buried the mouse and the fledgling in a border in the garden. We stared up towards the attic and saw the owls, lit by moonlight now, flying in with more meat for their young.

'The builders'll be coming soon,' said Mina. 'I'll make sure they do nothing until the chicks have flown.'

Forty-five

That Saturday the builders came to sort the garage out. There were three of them, an old man in a cap, Mr Batley, and his two sons, Nick and Gus. They thumped the walls and watched them sway and tremble. They heard the roof creaking and sagging. They scratched the bricks and watched them flake easily away. They yanked Dad's planks off and peered inside.

Mr Batley took his cap off and scratched his bald head.

'Wouldn't get me in there for danger money,' he said.

He pondered. He shrugged and twisted his mouth and looked at Dad.

'Know what I'm going to say, don't you?' he said.

'Suppose so,' said Dad.

'Nowt else for it. Knock it down and start again.'

Dad looked at me.

'What d'you think?' he said.

'Don't know,' I said.

'Easy choice,' said Mr Batley. 'Knock it down or sit and watch it fall down.'

Dad laughed.

'Go on, then,' he said. 'Get the stuff out from inside and knock it down.'

They put steel props up to keep the roof from falling in while they worked inside. They brought the junk out and laid it around Ernie's toilet in the wilderness: all the ancient chests of drawers, the broken washbasins, the bags of cement, the broken doors, the tattered deckchairs, rotted carpets, the ropes, the pipes, the newspapers and magazines, the coils of cable, the bags of nails. Dad and I went through it all as they brought it out. We kept saying, 'This'll come in useful,' then saying, 'No, it won't, it's just a piece of junk.' A truck came and left a huge steel skip in the back lane. We chucked in everything. We were all covered in dead bluebottles, dead spiders, brick and mortar dust. When it was empty, we stood around drinking tea and laughing at the mess.

I went to the door alone and stared in.

'Michael!' said Dad.

'Yes,' I said. 'I know. I won't go in.'

He told the builders about how desperate I'd been to get in there after we'd moved in.

'Just like these two used to be,' said Mr Batley. 'Show them something dark and dangerous and it was the devil's own work to keep them out.'

I kept on staring. Just rubble and dust and broken pottery, and in the far corner a couple of takeaway trays, some brown ale bottles, a scattered handful of feathers, the pellets. I sighed and whispered, 'Goodbye, Skellig.'

Then the builders and Dad were at my back.

'See,' said Mr Batley, pointing past me. 'Looks like you've had a dosser spending a night or two in there. Lucky the whole lot didn't come down on his head.'

Then we finished the tea. Mr Batley rubbed his hands.

'Right, then, lads,' he said. 'Time for a bit of knocky down.'

It only took an hour or two. We stood in the kitchen and watched them work with crowbars and sledgehammers and saws. We bit our lips and shook our heads each time a bit of roof or a bit of wall fell with a massive thump. Soon the garage was just a great pile of bricks and timber and dust.

'Bloody hell,' said Dad.

'Least we'll have a nice long garden for the baby to play in,' I said.

He nodded, and started talking about the lawn he'd lay, and the pond he'd dig, and the shrubs he'd plant for the birds to build their nests in.

'Ha!' he said. 'A little paradise for us all.'

When it was over, Gus and Nick stood proud and happy with their hands on their hips. Mr Batley, white as death with dust, gave us the thumbs up and we went out with more tea.

'Bloody lovely, that was,' he said.

'Aye,' said Gus. 'You cannot beat a bit of knocky down.'

Forty-six

She came home on a Sunday. A beautiful bright warm day. It was really spring at last. Dad went off in the car and I stayed behind to finish cleaning the kitchen up. I wrapped last night's takeaway tins in newspaper and threw them in the bin. I put the kettle on for Mum. I got a can of beer and a glass ready for Dad.

I went upstairs and slipped the baby's feather under her mattress. I smiled, because I knew she'd have the best of dreams.

I waited, looking out into the empty space left by Mr Batley and his sons. Even the cracked concrete floor was gone now. There was a wooden fence instead of the back wall. I imagined the garden, filled it with all the shrubs and flowers and the grass that would soon be growing where the wilderness had been.

I trembled when I heard the car. I couldn't move. Then I took deep breaths, and thought of Skellig and went to open the front door. Dad had the baby in his arms. Mum stood there beaming.

'Welcome home, Mum,' I whispered, using the words I'd practised.

She smiled at how nervous I was. She took my hand and led me back into the house, into the kitchen. She sat me on a chair and put the baby in my arms.

'Look how beautiful your sister is,' she said. 'Look how strong she is.'

I lifted the baby higher. She arched her back as if she was about to dance or fly. She reached out, and scratched with her tiny nails at the skin on my face. She tugged at my lips and touched my tongue. She tasted of milk and salt and of something mysterious, sweet and sour all at once. She whimpered and gurgled. I held her closer and her dark eyes looked right into me, right into the place where all my dreams were, and she smiled.

'She'll have to keep going for check-ups,' Mum said. 'But they're sure the danger's gone, Michael. Your sister is really going to be all right.'

We laid the baby on the table and sat around her. We didn't know what to say. Mum drank her tea. Dad let me have swigs of his beer. We just sat there looking at each other and touching each other and we laughed and laughed and we cried and cried.

Soon, there was a gentle knock at the door. I went and found Mina standing there. She was shy and quiet, like I'd never seen her before. She started to say something, but it was a mumble and she ended up just looking into my eyes.

'Come and see,' I said.

I took her hand and led her into the kitchen. She said good evening politely to my parents. She said she hoped they didn't mind. Dad shifted aside to let her in beside the table. She looked down at the baby.

'She's beautiful,' she gasped. 'She's extraordinary!'

And she looked around and laughed with us all.

She was really shy again when she said, 'I brought a present. I hope you don't mind.'

She unrolled a picture of Skellig, with his wings rising from his back and a tender smile on his white face.

Mum caught her breath.

She stared at me and she stared at Mina. For a moment, I thought she was going to ask us something. Then she simply smiled at both of us.

'Just something I made up,' said Mina. 'I thought the baby might like it on her wall.'

'It's really lovely, Mina,' Mum said, and she took it gently from Mina's hands.

'Thank you,' said Mina. She stood there awkwardly. 'I'll leave you alone now.'

I led her back to the door.

We smiled at each other.

'See you tomorrow, Mina.'

'See you tomorrow, Michael.'

I watched her walk away in the late light. From across the street, Whisper came to join her. When Mina stooped down to stroke the cat, I was sure I saw for a second the ghostly image of her wings.

Back in the kitchen, they were talking again about giving the baby a proper name.

'Persephone,' I said.

'Not that mouthful again,' said Dad.

We thought a little longer, and in the end we simply called her Joy.